Automaton

T.R. Hudson

To AV, who always brings me home.

"Man is a creature that can get accustomed to anything, and I think that is the best definition of him."
- Fyodor Dostoevsky

CHAPTER ONE

They repainted the MRAP again. The armored vehicle had once been green, then tan, then black, and was now a light blue, complete with stenciled writing on the side like General Patton's ice cream truck.

"Protection at Home for Protection Abroad"

In his seat, Michael thought about the moving target that he rode in, wondering if the many layers of paint added any extra protection and the nonsense phrase that the marketing department came up with for them. The self-driving truck was a hodgepodge of replacement parts, welded sheets of scrap metals, a somewhat functional engine, and a guidance system based on maps that were ten years out of date. That Michael put a good chunk of his pay into the truck, along with all the gear he carried, was typical of his team and throughout all the recruitment teams of Deluge, Inc.

Michael thought about the briefing they got earlier. "Don't kill if you don't have to. If you need to shoot, try to wound them. Getting shot at does not permit you to shoot back." Same shit, different day. All these different ways of saying that he was expendable should have angered him, but he'd accepted the cold reality of his work much the same way one accepts bumper-to-bumper traffic or walking through rain without an umbrella. "It is what it is" was his mantra and he often repeated the tired cliché like it was his trigger phrase.

"Doesn't make a whole lot of sense, does it, Mike?" Gomez asked.

Michael gave a slight nod, hoping to stop the loudmouthed Gomez before another tirade. The dozens of stories he told couldn't all be bullshit and if even three or four were true, then he was lucky to still be alive and out there, luck counted more than anything else.

"I mean," Gomez complained, "who are we protecting when we knock in some old woman's door and snatch her grandson to go fight the rest of the fucking country. And since when is fucking California abroad? I lived in California when I was a kid. Seemed like anywhere else to me."

"Well it ain't no more, Slow-mez," replied Chief, slapping him on the back of the head. "If you'd have paid attention, you'd know that sixty-two percent of the population supports our mission when framed in terms of protection from internal and external threats."

Chief Axel was all Michael knew him as. No first name. No family. Not even sure if Axel was his real name. SEALs of his era took on call signs, something about security. Michael suspected this was a parlor trick divined from pure ego. They were arrogant like that. It was said that when Navy SEALs run into battle, not far behind were their publicists and ghostwriters. Fake names probably sold a lot of books and movie deals.

"Meaning, if we tell the public that the fugitives they are harboring are dangerous and the enemy outside our borders are dangerous, too, then they are more likely to comply and help us get troops on the front lines. Which means a heavier purse for us," Chief explained, settling the matter.

The engines started up and the MRAP rolled out of the basement garage of their headquarters, followed by a large tractor-trailer. Michael got up from the bench seats that lined the walls of the truck and looked out the small porthole window behind him, noticing the streets were empty that day and finding the quiet alarming.

Gomez started a story about one of the many women he'd been with. Chief paid him no mind, instead escaping into his book. They were always Romance novels, with the bare-chested Fabio's on the cover and a lustful woman hanging off his arm. No one said anything about it. Everyone has their preferences. Newbie listened to the story with great interest. Michael hadn't yet learned his name, Newbie didn't rate that yet. He'd been with them for eight months but he still acted like Bambi in the forest. But where Bambi ran away from gunfire, Newbie seemed drawn to it and he'd shown himself dependable when it counted. He'd earn a name soon enough.

As Gomez went on, Caroline rolled her eyes. There were only a few women in their sector, soldiering not the first choice most girls put down on Career day. She didn't say much and didn't react when the others would poke and prod her, hoping to get a rise out of her. She waited them out with quiet dignity, like those marble statues in the museums that Michael was forced to visit as a child. She was not attractive by most men's standards, but that stopped very few from trying to get in her pants. Gomez ended with a raunchy punchline, which got a laugh from everyone, even Chief. Donahue laughed the loudest. He always laughed loudest and first, even if what was said wasn't funny. He laughed even louder at things that weren't funny. He was imposing, though average in height, he cast a long shadow and a steely gaze that kept most everyone on his good side. Donahue was the type that tortured small animals as a kid and saw most everything as his plaything until he grew tired of them and that complicated the team dynamic they all strove to create out of professional necessity.

The convoy passed Chestnut street, where Michael's friends Bobby and Brandon lived when they were kids. They went to college on baseball scholarships when Michael enlisted. Bobby played a season for Cleveland before May Day. Later, they were drafted and Bobby died in the Appalachia Campaign. Brandon's body was never found, but they figured he was at the Siege of Fort Benning. The timeline fit, but there was never any way to confirm it. Rumor was, the retreat was so swift that even the wounded were left behind.

They reached the edge of Jersey City and were about to pass Checkpoint X, the last safe spot they'd see for some time. Michael got up from his seat and climbed up into the turret, manning the fifty-caliber machine gun that provided security for the convoy. The autonomous vehicle got from point A to point B well enough, but lack of proper maintenance, a pitiful budget for equipment, and a low value for human life meant that Michael's watchful eye was often the difference between life and death. As they passed the checkpoint, the guard on the ground gave him a friendly wave and a smile, which Michael did not return, let alone acknowledge.

A couple of hours passed and the truck crossed over an old metal girder bridge and a loud crunch was heard and the whole vehicle jumped. Michael tried to see what they'd hit, but the truck didn't slow and there were more important things to look out for. All he saw was a fog hanging over the river and a blown-up toll booth, whose E-Z pass sign seemed to flash on and off, though that was impossible.

"I'm going to do a weapons test", Michael called over the radio.

"Okay", Chief grumbled. It seemed Michael interrupted another joke, the word buzz-kill was thrown around him more than once. He didn't like jokes. There was nothing funny about what was going on and even in the days that he could laugh, he doubted there was much to laugh about. He fired twenty-one rounds in three round bursts into the sides of buildings, knocking away the brick, steel, and concrete that were once homes and businesses. He put three rounds in an old car, hitting the gas tank and causing an explosion.

It was another hour before they got to their sector. The neighborhood used to be a few cul-de-sacs with large houses on wide stretches of property, covered in grass and trees and tacky lawn ornaments. Michael's father used to call these McMansions, assembled off the line, piece by piece with inferior materials, without craft or care. Many winters sagged the roofs of a few and almost all the windows were broken in every house. The once pristine, manicured lawns were replaced with cardboard shantytowns.

Any open space was converted to gardens, even if they never grew anything. The land wasn't barren, as wildflowers and weeds bloomed most everywhere else, but since the fall, the green thumbs either headed West, died, or faded away. Michael was used to this kind of thing by now. The people lucky enough to live in the houses fit three to four families in a room. Latrine pits were set up at the mouth of the neighborhood and the smell of burning excrement spread carcinogens to people who wouldn't live long enough to die of cancer but would have to live every moment with a nose full of burnt shit. Their truck and the Semi crawled up to the center-of-circle and Michael and the others unloaded.

"What the hell did we roll into?" Newbie asked.

"Refugee camp of sorts," Michael replied. "Just keep your eyes open and the radio channel clear."

"Okay, Mike. If you say so."

"Relax. Turn on if you have to. These people can smell fear. A whiff of that and you're fucked."

"I'm good. I don't use that stuff unless I need it."

Lucky bastard, Michael thought.

Chief grabbed his megaphone, climbed up next to the turret, and spoke aloud.

"Good Afternoon, my name is Chief Axel. We are from the Bureau of Military Affairs, Recruitment and Acquisitions, a subsidiary of Deluge World Wide. Today, we are here to clear your neighborhood and find the dangerous individuals who are making life unsafe for all of us. Your cooperation in this matter will be greatly appreciated and allow us to get out of your way quicker."

Chief, standing on top of the truck, covered head to toe in body armor and brandishing a complement of weapons, looked like an executioner but sounded like a Walmart greeter.

"Donahue, Connors", Chief called into the channel, "Go to the head shed and talk to the HOH. Remember, be diplomatic in there. We don't have enough bodies or ammo. Newbie, take Mike's place in the Crow's nest."

The Main house had a two car garage and the only window that wasn't boarded up was the basement window on the side closest to the cul-de-sac's neck. It was the only house with a lawn, yellow and brown in most spots, but freshly mowed. A goat tied to a post was chewing on grass. On one each of the boards, in spray paint, read the neighborhood's laws.

1. No stealing from Arlo.

2. No touching Arlo's women.

3. Arlo's word is law.

After circling the property, feeling the eyes inside on him, Michael went to the front door and knocked, Donahue, covering him from the sidewalk. An emaciated child answered the door.

"My name is Connors. I'm looking for a few people who skipped their draft day. Can I speak to whoever's in charge?"

The small child looked like he could have been anywhere from eight to fifteen. It was tough to pin considering how horrid and dirty he was. Michael wasn't even entirely sure he was a boy or one of "Arlo's women".

"Arlo is this way, Rep," the child said. Michael entered the house, checking for any surprises, booby traps, or kill holes from the second floor. After clearing the front room, he popped back outside to signal that it was okay to enter. Donahue came in, did his own check and then the pair followed the boy up the stairs to meet whoever Arlo was. Outside the master bedroom, stood a short, stocky man with a deep scar on one cheek and a spear made from an old, wooden coat rack and a kitchen knife duct-taped at the end. Michael thought it looked ridiculous, but if he wasn't armed, hadn't eaten much in a while, and lived like an animal the way these people were living, he was sure that the spear would give him pause. The child didn't notice the spear and spoke to the guard as one would to a co-worker. The guard looked Michael and Donahue up and down, then opened the door, announcing their presence to Arlo.

"Arlo, these Reps are here for our people."

Arlo, who was laying in a California King Bed, naked as the day he was born, and surrounded by ten equally naked women on the bed, sat up to receive the two recruiters. He took no action to cover himself, instead forcing everyone to see his naked body. He had the remnants of a more muscular frame, hairless and a few shades shy of midnight black. His manhood on display was not the spectacle that would usually warrant a crowd, but Arlo stood proud, projecting aloof confidence as if he was daring someone to call him out. Michael guessed that

11

those who did were given swift retribution and chose to make no mention of it.

"Gentlemen, welcome to my home. My name is Arlo and these are my friends," he said, motioning to the women laying on the bed, who met them with shy looks and giggles. "You've already met Rodney, the head of home security, as well as Anthony, the ward of the estate. Megan, could you please bring a couple glasses of water for our guests."

One of the women, a short blonde, who looked well fed compared to most of the other people in the neighborhood, got up and walked into the master bathroom. Her long lochs covered her reduced bosom and though it was clear she'd lost weight, she maintained her curves and childbearing hips. She returned a few moments later with two full glasses. Michael took the glass out of politeness. Donahue drank the whole glass in front of everyone as if he'd just finished a marathon, letting several drops hit the ground. Michael noticed the boy, Anthony, looked at every spilled drop with anger and wanting as the three wet spots slowly dried into the carpet.

"Refreshing, thanks", Donahue humored, " Now, are you the homeowner?"

"I am indeed. Are you surprised? Is it shocking to see a black man own a home in this day and age?"
"No, it's just that," Donahue started.

"We saw the windows. Figured that whoever owned the signs wouldn't be so… articulate," Michael stepped in.

"Smooth, Rep. Very smooth. Some people around here are as sharp as snowballs, so I keep the rules quite simple. I'm sure even you could follow them".

Donahue motioned towards his rifle, but Michael cut in before anything happened that couldn't be taken back.

"Now, we have a list of names we'd like you to go through and see if you can identify any of them. Any name you give us can be exchanged for credits. D-Coins. Worth more than gold, at least that's what the tickers say."

"Look around, Rep. Do you see any open D-Marts nearby? Is there a new aid station that I'm not aware of? Flip a switch anywhere in the house, there's no power. If you haven't noticed, Crypto is useless here and I need my people. I need guards to keep my water safe from thieves. My neighbors are always looking for weaknesses to exploit. I need my women to warm my bed at night. I get cold and lonely so easily. My people aren't going with you."

Arlo stood firm, hints of laughter coming from the guards and the women. Donahue looked annoyed Michael stone faced.

"Okay, fine, for every body you identify, I'll trade you a quarter box of FedRats. Think of it this way. More food for your household and less mouths to feed," Donahue replied.

Arlo got up from the bed and put on his robe, a pink bathrobe with purple polka dots, then walked towards the two recruiters. He towered over both of them and stared them down. Neither man blinked and a genial smile came over Arlo's face. He stretched out a hand towards them.

"Half box," he replied and Donahue accepted, shaking Arlo's hand in regal fashion. "Though, I doubt anyone of my people are lawbreakers. My people are good and honest citizens. My neighbors across the main road, however, are a different story. You'll have more luck over there."

It was the same everywhere. Roll into one village to go fuck another. As soon as Arlo said that, Michael knew they'd be going home with a full load.

"You might be right," Donahue replied with a smirk, "but in that case, we're going to need your help rounding them up."

"Naturally. What kind of citizen would I be if I ignored my duty to my country?" Arlo replied, with more laughs coming from the gallery. Donahue put a map on the bed, and Arlo began explaining the defenses the neighborhood across the street had. Arlo explained that his men would feint a frontal assault, when another guard burst into the room, frenzied with excitement.

"Arlo!" the man yelled, "We've got him!."

Arlo pulled his attention off of the war plans.

"Where is he?"

"We've got him in the backyard, ready for you."

Arlo turned his attention back to Michael and Donahue.

"Excuse me, Gentlemen. I have more pressing business."

"Hey!", Donahue yelled, "We didn't have to be as cordial as we have been. We can do this another way real fucking quick." Donahue then moved his hand to the rifle slung across his body.

The two guards pointed their spears at Donahue's neck, while Michael drew down on Arlo with cold indifference.

"Trevor, Deandre, lower your weapons. Donahue, please understand, someone has been siphoning water from my aqueduct and that's been causing me all kinds of headaches. I can be much more useful to you if you allow me to first take care of this small business."

Donahue took his hand off the rifle and Michael lowered his.

"You're the boss, Arlo. But, don't jerk me around."

"Thank you. And after, I'll shower you in derelicts."

Arlo led his guards, the two recruiters, plus a few of the women downstairs and out the back door. All through the house were other guards, other women who were noticeably malnourished, as well as a handful of children running around. The backyard was mostly converted into garden planters, surrounded by a six foot wooden fence, reinforced with a variety of different kinds of scrap metals like street signs, old refrigerators, and other appliances, and anything else that could keep Arlo's neighbors out of his property.

Two burly guards, carrying similar makeshift spears flanked a skinny, shirtless man, whose unkempt beard and showing ribs made it look like he'd be stranded on some desert island. His skin was burned by the sun's harsh rays on several parts of his

15

body and his swollen brown eyes strained from too much crying. Bruises lined his sides and arms, which he wrapped around his body, shaking himself forward and back, muttering 'I'm sorry' over and over again.

Arlo walked over the beaten man and raised his head to see his face.

"Who sent you to steal my water? Was it Tom Andrews? Roger? Annette down the street?"

"No one. I was just thirsty."

Arlo slapped the man across the face. He wore a few rings that tore into the man's already bloodied skin, cutting deep gashes into him as the blood that had built up in welts burst like water balloons onto the ground below.

"I hate liars. Do you see those tomato plants in the corner there? The shriveled up ones that look like they could really use a drink?" He grabbed the man's head and turned it towards the garden.

"They wouldn't be that way if someone had only taken a few drinks of my water. You've stolen at least ten gallons over the last week, I figure. Who did you steal them for?"

"No one, I swear!"

Just short of licking his lips, Donahue looked like he was going to need a few moments alone as Arlo continued to beat the man. Like a shark in frenzy, Donahue cultivated an aura around himself whenever blood was spilled that could best be described as primitive lust. Writhing on the ground, the man could barely get any words out. He tried to scream, but only a whisper could come out and the bizarre sight of a man whispering for his life made Arlo laugh.

"There exists about one and a half gallons of blood in a human being, thief. Tell me who sent you so I can get another eight and a half back from them!"

"Roger," he whispered. "Roger sent me. Please, don't kill me. Please, I want to live. I'm sorry. Please."

Arlo, satisfied, put his hand out as one of the guards brandished a hunting knife and placed the handle in Arlo's open palm. Arlo walked over and grabbed the man by his matted hair, manipulating him so that his chin was up as he placed the blade across the thief's neck.

"Before May Day, I worked in finance," Arlo declared. "I used to commute to the city every day and I made money hand over fist. But it never gave me any satisfaction. Not any real satisfaction, anyway."

Arlo danced the knife around the thief's neck, as small bits of his beard fell to the ground into the pool of blood below, looking like rowboats in a crowded pond.

"But now, I have a small kingdom. I'm responsible for every action that occurs on my land. I took a political science course in college, we talked about the state's monopoly on violence. It was the cornerstone of law and order. Today, I am that law. And the monopoly is mine. And I take immense satisfaction from that."

Donahue was sweating, speechless, watching with an intensity usually reserved for hyenas, vultures, and other scavenging animals. Michael watched on with no emotion one way or the other. It was what it was in his mind. But, then, a thought occurred to him, causing him to shout out.

"Wait. What is his name?"

Arlo looked over, annoyed. Donahue was visibly frustrated, blue balled.

"What does that matter?", Arlo asked.

"If he's on my list, then he's worth more to both of us alive."

Arlo thought it over for a moment, then removed the knife from the thief's neck, wearing a devilish smile.

"Very well, he's yours if he's on there."

The man, who could barely whisper, tried with all his might to speak, but couldn't. Michael decided a different approach.

"Nod if you hear your name. Abu Nasir Ali."

The man, who most certainly was not Abu Nasir Ali, with all his might, shook his head as if he wasn't at all injured. Satisfied, Michael looked at Arlo to gauge his reaction. He had a stern look on his face for a moment before smiling wide.

"Wonderful! Now that that is taken care of, let's see what other trash I can have taken out."

Arlo formed up his men, about twenty, into a neat formation. Arlo himself took out a pistol that looked as if it had never been fired. It was a nickel plated, forty-five caliber M1911 with custom grips and an imposing shine. On the side, engraved over the slide, were the words "Ultima Ratio Regum". Michael was spying it and Arlo approached him before they set off on the short march across the desolate street that divided the two miniature kingdoms.

"You know any Latin, Connors?"

"No."

"In France, King Louis XIV built a massive palace as a testament to his greatness. Versailles, ever heard of it?"

Michael nodded.

"He lined the outer walls with cannons and inscribed on them were the words 'Ultima Ratio Regum'. The last argument of Kings."

They caught Roger and his neighborhood by surprise. There was little resistance. The men and women selected went in willingly, most looked half-starved and probably wouldn't survive training, but that was of no concern. The recruiters were paid by the body. The new recruits got used to their new names quickly but were then told their service numbers would prove to be more important. Deluge had a new unit of soldiers destined to bring the country back together again. Arlo, getting his justice, executed Roger and several others. Donahue was pleased. Michael saw a few women segregated away from the rest. Arlo would have a few more bed warmers for the cold nights ahead.

Chief gathered the team around before heading back, a wide smile on his face, matched by most of the others, save for Michael.

"Good work today, people," Chief declared. "Sixty-Three Americans for the cause. Drinks are on them tonight."

"Gracie Pub?" Gomez asked.

"Where else?" Caroline asked.

Finally, Abu Nasir was loaded into the truck, laying on a makeshift stretcher. With the little strength he could muster, he called out to Michael, beckoning him over before the doors were shut.

"Thank you for saving my life," he struggled to get out.

"All I did was delay the inevitable, *Abu*."

Michael was about to close the door to the Semi when one of Arlo's guards came towards him.

"I'd like to go, too. I'm on the list."

"What's your name?"

"Whatever name you haven't called yet."

"Trust me, you're better off here. You have food, shelter, and from what I saw, more than enough incentive to stick around. You don't want to go."

"As soon as you leave, shits gonna hit the fan. There's gonna be a war. Arlo pissed off a lot of his neighbors and doesn't have enough strength to fight them all himself. Is it really worse there than it'll get here? I doubt it. At least with the army, I'll have a gun. Here, I've got a fucking stick and a knife."

Michael looked him up and down, waiting for him to waver, but no such weakness came. His mind was made up. Michael stared at the list, looking for an unclaimed name, "Paul Reed. Service Number 328078996."

"Paul Reed," the man replied as he climbed into the back of the truck. Michael closed the door behind him.

The trucks left the cul-de-sac, having enough bodies for the day to be considered a good haul. Michael, taking his spot in the turret watched as the night sky was obscured by rising black smoke from back the way they came. He wondered if Paul Reed was correct. Arlo acted untouchable, but there was always a bigger fish. If they'd rolled into Roger's territory, it would have been Arlo's head instead. But that didn't matter. There had been a hundred Arlos and hundreds more to come. Each of them content with their small kingdoms and each of them would be toppled in an afternoon if the price was right. "It is what it is", Michael murmured as they reached the highway towards home.

CHAPTER TWO

The Gracie Pub, established in 1990, was by all accounts a shit hole dive bar. None of the toilet stalls had doors, not even in the women's room. The beer was usually warm and if there was food, it was always served cold. The bartender, who everyone just called Tim, had not one hair on his body and was missing an eye. He never talks about it, in fact, he never talks. Rumor was that it was gouged out in a bar fight by a tweaker who couldn't pay his tab. Tim must have hated wearing a patch, deciding to just let people see the gaping hole that his left eye once resided in. Anyone who couldn't stand to look at him wasn't welcome anyway, which made it a perfect place for recruiters, who'd all lost pieces of themselves long before.

"Timmy," Caroline shouted as the door burst open and the team of recruiters flooded to their usual table in the back. "A round of the top shelf for us."

"Only the best tonight. Whiskey," Chief shouted.

"Just water for me", Newbie replied, getting dirty looks from the rest, save for Michael, who didn't care. Tim brought the drinks.

Sitting at the bar with an old fedora was a short man with thick-rimmed glasses. He must have thought looked dashing as he wore the beat-up hat indoors and was otherwise unremarkable. He kept his eyes off the bunch and they paid him no mind, except Donahue, who couldn't keep his eyes off the small man of no consequence. He wore that same look of lust and desperation that he had at Arlo's, the way a tiger looks at a lamb.

An hour or so passed and Tim kept the drinks coming, and the team of hardened recruiters got rowdy. Gomez was cursing in Spanish while Donahue sang love songs no one had heard of or at least had forgotten. Caroline talked of getting 'white girl wasted', which only drew disgust from the others save for Donahue. Their revelry annoyed Michael, who only came because the drinks were cheapest here and if he drank enough, he could feel the impressions of feelings that he remembered long ago. Another round came around, including the water for Newbie, which only brought on more cajoling from the others, who now existed in a steady buzz.

"Come on, Newb, just one. We're a team, after all," Gomez reasoned.

"I can't. I don't believe in it."

"Well, it's here. It's real. You believing in it or not doesn't change that," Caroline replied.

"I'm a Mormon." The rest rolled their eyes. Even Michael passed some judgment. Caroline made a puking sound. Donahue shifted attention from the man at the bar to Newbie, bewildered by his admission.

"You wear the magic underpants?" Chief asked.

"Under my uniform, I wear the temple garments, yes."

"Did you wear them when you were in the service?"

"I did."

"You ever piss your magic underpants? Like, when an IED went off, or when you took rounds? It's okay if you did. I remember Persia. I pissed my pants. Everyone does. I know a guy who shit himself. No shame in it."

"My first deployment, I was intel. I didn't take any rounds before I got the ETP. You were in a long time before the surgery, huh, Chief?"

"Twenty-five years in the Navy. Master Chief Petty Officer Axel. US Navy SEALS. At your service, Newbie."

"Shit, you must have been the guinea pigs for ETP, huh?" Gomez butted in.

"Back then, they called it BALANCE. Don't ask me what it stood for, but yeah, we were the first. The original idea was to keep Special Operations on longer rotations without side effects. Lotta good SEALS went nuts doing deployments back to back like that. So BALANCE was a way to keep us sharp and well, balanced. Once they perfected it and realized the wider implications, they repackaged it and offered it to every GI Joe wannabe who could hold a pen. When I retired, the admin clerk who signed off on my paperwork had ETP. Now anyone can be a badass like me."

"I heard it was a CIA project," Gomez added. "Cold War tech. They took normal people, scrambled their brains, and when they heard the trigger phrase, boom, stone cold killer. MK Ultra shit."

Caroline rolled her eyes. "You would believe in conspiracies you stupid fuck."

"Fuck you, bitch", he yelled. "At least I'm not some walking mattress diversity hire. How does Donahue's dick taste, Puta?"

It was no secret that they'd shacked up before, but no one had put it in the open. Even if they were Mr. and Mrs. Cleaver, no one would care. The days of HR seminars and sexual harassment were long gone. Justice was reserved for the most heinous acts and most times, it was never served.

"Why don't you ask your mother? Or is she too busy shooting up to answer these days?"

Gomez burst out laughing, almost spilling his beer. He was a ballbuster, but if you could take it and dish it, he mostly left you alone. Newbie was his favorite target, but then, getting shit on was his job.

"Yeah yeah yeah," Gomez dismissed, then changed the subject. "What's your trigger phrase, old man? Help, I've fallen and I can't get up!?" which drew laughter from most everyone else.

"Fuck you," Chief laughed. "If you must know, I use the lyrics of the great Warrior Poet DMX. Break bread with my enemy, but no matter how many cats I break bread with, I'll break who you sendin' me."

Chief's eyes opened wide, his pupils shrunk and his veins popped out like his blood boiled in an instant. He was scanning the room, looking for threats, and when he saw it was clear, he still kept up the defense. His breathing was steady and on the surface he was calm. He repeated the lyrics and came back down. Turned off from his heightened state.

Applause came from around the table. "Wow, they really fucked you up, huh?" Gomez chided. "I mean, you look like the goddamn hulk."

Chief laughed, looking content. Deep scaring on his arms and most notably on his neck showed all who could see that many had tried to kill him and none succeeded. Michael remembered on his first day, Chief telling him that he enjoyed being a bad motherfucker.

"What's your's Newb? 'My name is the Lord and I shall lay my vengeance upon you'?" Gomez chided.

Newbie looked dumbfounded. "I haven't heard that verse before." Caroline shook her head.

"Well if Tarantino isn't your guy, then who is?" Chief asked.

Donahue left the table, walking over to the man alone at the bar.

"I remember when I was a kid, at the end of a service, we'd all say this goodbye thing. My mother told me that Brigham Young used to say it at the end of all meetings and it caught on from there. It was about getting back safely and when I was overseas, all I thought about was my wife and our kids and how I would get back to them. So when it came time to choose words, the only thing that felt right was, 'Bless that we will travel home in safety'."

Newbie turned on, his innocent stare replaced with a hardened look of pure indifference. His wide blue eyes became sharp, piercing, dangerous, like icicles in the coldest winters. Newbie repeated his words, turning off, and banishing his Hyde to the deepest, most primordial parts of his mind. The innocent father of three returned, greeted by his peers.

"No wonder they call us Reps," Caroline said with an impressed approval.

"I never understood that," Newbie replied. "Reps? Representatives? Like we represent something? The government? Deluge?" The rest looked at him like adults to a child who made some unintentional faux pas.

"Reptile," Michael answered, then sipping his drink.

"I think it's badass. Like those flags with the snake. 'Don't Tread On Me" and all that shit," Gomez enthused. "Even though, every day, we tread and tread."

"Gomez, how the fuck did they even let you be a recruiter? All you ever talk about is how we're the bad guys or how we are doing some evil shit," Chief rebuked.

27

"We are doing some evil shit, Chief. You can't say we aren't. But, to me, it's necessary evil. Newbie's got his family. So do you. Mike's got his mom and Caroline, well I don't know shit about you, but I figure there's a whole house full of cats that would starve to death if you weren't there shaking the dry food bag."

"Your point?" Caroline asked.

"My point is that I've got people, too. Some are still in Arizona. Some are still in Mexico. The rest are in friendly territory. My point is, we gotta do some evil shit to prevent even more evil shit. I'm okay with that, but I'm just keeping it real. Everything else is a fucking fairytale."

Tim came by with another round, knowing that his best customers were ready for it. Michael looked over at the bar, seeing Donahue talking to the stranger with the hat. Donahue closed the distance between them, leaving little personal space. The man looked up, shocked after hearing what Donahue had whispered to him. The pair looked over to the table, Donahue no doubt referencing the group. Then, both men got up and walked outside, Donahue's arm around the meek man's shoulder. They left their drinks and the man left his hat on the bar top. Michael turned his attention back to the others as they tried to ask him something.

"So, Mike. What's your deal?" Gomez asked.

"Donahue just left with that man."

"Yeah, yeah," Gomez dismissed, "But what about your words?"

"My words?"

"Yeah, what do you do to turn on?"

"We gotta come up with another way to say that," Caroline insisted.

"I once fucked my ex-girlfriend while I was on. That shit was wild. Told me to fuck her doggie style since she couldn't take the look in my eye. She thought I was going to rip her head off," Gomez replied.

"Amazing that it didn't work out, Chief interjected.

"Yeah, her sister was pretty hot, and I was about to get deployed, so I shot my shot. Worth every shot she took at me."

"My wife is way prettier than her sisters", Newbie added under his breath.

"Who the fuck asked, Newbie?" Gomez shot back. "Unless you're gonna give me an in with some of that sweet, virgin pussy, shut the fuck up."

"I was just saying," Newbie urged, withdrawing. "Besides, most of them are still in Salt Lake City."

"No need to talk about the Man's family, Slow-mez," Chief jeered. "Connors was about to divulge his most closely guarded secret. Sergeant Connors, the floor is yours,"

Michael sat and thought for a moment. All he ever did was sit quietly. He wondered if he should lie. Lying would have been easier, but there was no real point. It changed nothing, just made him talk more which he was loathe to do. The truth was complicated, but that described most of his life. He looked back across the room and there, standing, was Sergeant Ross, his arms folded and his disappointment radiated out from his power stance. He hadn't shown up for a few days. He'd appear once in a while in a crowd of recruits or the background of a movie or show. Most of the time he just stood there, looking indignant, the same pissed off look he had at every formation, mandatory function, and dog and pony show. The man was immune to joy, even in death.

"Lying is the opiate of weak men, Corporal," was all Michael heard before turning his attention back to the team.

"I don't know," he answered, though everyone else seemed to have forgotten what he was answering. The others couldn't quite grasp what he said, sharing confused looks across the table. "I forgot my words. I was on patrol and we got blown up. I woke up in a hospital and forgot a lot. I got most of it back, but I couldn't remember my words."

"So you haven't turned on in like, what, eleven years?" Gomez asked.

"I haven't turned off in twelve years, three months, thirteen days, and six hours."

"Ho-ly Shit," Chief responded. "I thought you were just a fucking psycho like Donahue."

"You really are a goddamn reptile? What's it like?" Gomez asked. "I mean, I know what it's like, but I was never on for more than a few hours or so. And I was exhausted afterward."

"How do you sleep?" Caroline asked.

"Poorly. I get maybe three hours a night, once every few days or so. There's no real schedule to it. Doctors said I'm fine. One was surprised I slept at all. Told me I should be good without it entirely, but I try to anyway. Makes me feel... alive, I guess."

It was the first time he'd said it out loud. He thought it would bring him some peace, some sort of completeness, but instead, he was just as he'd been before. He might have even been the same if he'd lied. As a child, he felt bad for lying, but now, felt it was the only way to exist in a world where the truth had gone extinct, or at the very least, was in deep hibernation.

"I had my shit written down and pinned inside my kevlar for that very reason," Caroline insisted.

"My unit had a strict policy against it," Michael responded. "My squad leader had a way of knowing when things were unsat."

"Every unit did," Chief added, "Even in the SEAL teams and they're more relaxed than most. Didn't you watch the Thomas Tape?"

Michael remembered the Thomas Tape when he went to get his surgery. Some sailor, Salvatore Thomas, got captured when his patrol boat was raided by a Quds Force detachment. They killed every man on the boat, except for Thomas. The torture went on for thirty-six hours, ranging from psychological to the worst beating a man could endure. But he did endure all of this without changing his facial expression. They found his trigger phrase written in a bible he kept on him and when they turned him off, the shock from all his pain centers going off at once killed him on the spot. The order was standing from then on out, do not write down the trigger phrase.

"Yeah, we were forced to watch it," Caroline replied, fidgeting with her glass. "I'm not saying I was right, but well, I made through alright and without being lobotomized, so who's the real idiot?"

"I'm not complaining or blaming. It is what it is. This life is better than no life at all. For now at least."

The others sat in silence, drinking and contemplating. Michael felt no relief in letting the truth out to his teammates. He felt the same neutrality he had before. The quiet broke as Donahue marched back in, triumphant. Behind him, the short man slunk back to his seat. His glasses were crooked and his suit was in disarray. He laid down a credit card, collected his things, and left in a hurry, limping out the door. Donahue, all smiles, sat back in his spot, beaming.

"What's with all the sour faces? I'm gone fifteen minutes and I come back to a funeral. Hey, Timmy, another round of shots," he yelled to the stoic cyclops, who nodded and began pouring.

"What'd you do to him?" Caroline asked.

"I got laid. We went to his car. Nice car, too. Mercedes. Or a Beamer. I don't know, something German. Smooth leather interior. That stank ain't comin' out soon, I tell you that," he laughed, slapping Newbie on the back, who winced in return.

"I had no idea you were a fag," Gomez teased.

"Who said I was? I didn't fuck him cause he was a guy. I fucked him cause," Donahue stopped, the gears turning in his eyes. " I fucked him because I wanted to and that's all."

"Lucky for you that he was into it," Chief said with dismissal.

"Took some doing. He wasn't about it at all when I first started talking to him. But after a minute, I was able to persuade him. A little ass pain doesn't seem like much compared to getting sent out West." Donahue laughed and laughed, his jovial attitude poisoning the rest as looks of disgust came across the others. Michael, though he found it distasteful, took it all in stride. It was what it was.

"What?" Donahue asked. "Like you never leaned into someone to get something?"

"You really are a fucking psycho, Donahue," Chief spat.

"It's his own goddamn fault. Motherfucker walks around like that and he's just inviting trouble. Maybe now he'll know not to be so fucking weak. The whole goddamn world's gone to shit. Every man for himself and I aim to get mine, you get me?"

There were more disgusted looks around the table.

"Whatever. You guys can scold me and shun me, but you're no better. You might think you are, but deep down you all know you aren't. You all know that you make up names or threaten or whatever to make quotas. All I did was give a guy a chance to keep his life. I guarantee that there are thousands who'd take that deal every goddamn day. So don't you judge me, just because I'm out here trying to get mine while everyone else is getting theirs. We don't live in the world anymore. No more law. No more right. There's just the fuckers and the fucked."

Tim came around and placed the shots in front of each of them. The dark brown whiskey sat in each glass, unmolested until Donahue took his and drank. He placed the glass faced down and scanned across the table, waiting for the others to join him. Gomez raised his glass and took the shot. Caroline surprised them when she took hers. Chief, for all of his righteous indignation, drank with the rest. Newbie looked around the table for sympathy but was only met with contempt. Donahue started his stare down again until the Mormon lifted the glass to his lips, sipping slow and making a face of disgust, leaving Michael as the sole hold out.

"Is what it is," he said, putting the glass to his lips and tipping backward. The alcohol burned in his mouth and down his throat, unable to settle in his stomach.

They left the bar around three. Michael headed out into the darkness, taking a left as the others went right. An old car parked on the bar's left side was the only sign of life down the foreboding alley that Michael took to get home on many occasions. As he passed the car he heard a small whimper from behind. He noticed the man from the bar sitting on the ground, holding himself and crying. His left hand was extended, holding onto the driver-side door handle.

"P-please. D-don't hurt me. I-I gave him what he wanted. Just leave me alone. Please."

"I'm not going to hurt you."

"That's what he said." The man paused, "He lied."

"Why did you go with him?"

"He told me what you were. He told me that you'd recruit me and that I'd die out there for sure and that no one would care and that he was the only person who could do anything about it." The man was about the hyperventilate, then put his head in his hands.

"I'm sure that he did," Michael replied with cold dismissal.

"I have a family. Kids. He took all the credits I had after it was over. And I let him. I think that's the worst part. I let him do all of it. I didn't fight it. I should have." He started sobbing again. The streetlight down the alley made shadows of them along with the buildings, exaggerating his movements along the bar's outer wall like a puppet.

"But you didn't."

This made the man only cry more. He raised his face to get some air, escaping the smothering comfort of his hands, revealing the bloody, beaten face that Donahue left him with. Shards from his glasses were embedded in different spots around his face. The frames sat crooked on his nose, just as useful as the man was himself. Michael was sure that there were other such wounds all along the man's body. He sat, rocking back and forth, muttering to himself. Michael took a few steps back, straightening himself out.

"It could be worse," he thought. "I could be him." He left the man in that alley, curled up in agony, screaming like a wounded animal.

CHAPTER THREE

The lightest touches of sunlight, and the dawn that followed, beat Michael back to his apartment. On entering, the pungent smell of settled smoke attacked his senses. Before the war, this neighborhood was one of the nicer ones that Jersey City had to offer. People paid thousands per month to live in these shoe boxes because it was where everyone wanted to be. Now there were hardly any shoes to fill them and no one to come around asking for rent. The dark, narrow hallway that monopolized a decent portion of the studio apartment's meager square footage was lit with the faint flashes of the television in the living room.

There, sitting in her lounge chair, feet propped up and head nodded to sleep. Her mouth agape as the loud snores she wheezed out let Michael know that she was still alive. When there wasn't wheezing, there was coughing. The coughs of a much older, weaker woman. She wasn't very old but looked frail and infirmed. Michael found the late-night her most tolerable moments, where he was free from her ire and constant complaining. She was his mother and some deep-seated devotion to that relationship kept her in his life.

The apartment's walls were bare, except for a few pictures and the yellow stained cobwebs that lay in every corner. The paint, which was once eggshell, now equally stained a light, disturbing yellow, which emanated from where the woman sat and spread like a disease through the apartment. Michael thought of the gas drills he used to do and often wondered if he should buy a gas mask for himself. The station had plenty and he was sure that he could take one without being seen, but that kind of antagonizing would only lead to further escalation on her part. Every day was a little war of attrition, where both of them waited for the other to die so they could move on with their lives. He didn't hate her. But he didn't love her. Or he at least felt nothing warm towards her. He couldn't feel anything towards her. Or anyone else for that matter.

Michael, still buzzed from the night's events, stumbled to a cot he set up in the corner of the room and tried to sleep. Michael looked for earplugs, the dollar store kind that was sold by the bunch. He'd run out and with them ran away his chances of sleeping that night. He used to use sleeping pills, but they were in short supply near them, a luxury he couldn't afford and did not need. For a few moments, he thought about how he wouldn't need the plugs if she would only do something about the snoring. Then, after a few more quiet moments, he noticed a void in her coughing and wheezing. He walked over to check her pulse, unsure at that moment if he would save her life or let her die. He thought the idea disturbing but still thought it, arguing slightly for and against at once. As he stood over her, he noticed her mouth close and she, breathing out her nose. This respite ended soon after and the bombardment began again. Michael noticed that she had no blanket, so grabbed one from the basket next to her and covered her from the shoulders to her feet. He noticed the burn marks that permeated the blanket, like old pieces of parchment paper or swiss cheese. How anyone could live like this astounded Michael, but he then realized that he too was living like this. He thought about turning off the television but knew that it would only wake her.

A few more hours passed and Michael went to the kitchen, making powdered eggs on hardtack. His mother, still asleep, couldn't eat the hardtack and always insisted on having bacon, knowing that he would never be able to get it. Instead, the new impossible Fake-on had just hit store shelves. It tasted kind of like bacon if bacon were rubbery and tasted nothing like pork. The marketers who manufactured it must have banked on people forgetting what real bacon tasted like. Bacon. Electricity. Running water. These modern luxuries were once basic essentials. They'd gotten the lights back three years ago. He thought of a Deluge commercial, where a child was interviewed and asked what the most amazing thing he'd ever seen was. He answered, "I came home one day and I flipped a switch and the lights came on." They picked the most pathetic looking child they could find, one that would tug at the heartstrings. Deluge was the biggest company in the world, usurped the US government in exile. And still, they needed PR.

Michael finished making breakfast, the smell battling the other odors in the house. His mother caught a whiff, waking up in her usual mood.

"You were loud coming in last night."

He walked back to her with a TV tray full of food, placing it on her lap.

"No, I wasn't. I could have come right up to you and slit your throat before your eyes even had time to open."

He knew it was a lot, but this was war. What would have once shocked and dismayed her was only deflected by her hardened stare.

"I thought you'd died when you didn't come home."

"You'd have liked that, wouldn't you?"

She didn't answer, but he knew that she'd thought yes. Michael sat on his cot with his plate, wasting no time. He waited for her to finish and took the tray away, then started getting ready for work. A shower, shave, and fresh set of clothes was all he needed. His morning lasted an hour, tops. He walked into the bathroom and out of instinct, turned on the closest faucet to see that the water was running that day. Thirty-six days in a row. A new record.

The water that ran in that shower was scalding, reddening his skin as he stood under its pressured torrent. Emotions eluded him, but pain did not. Pain was real. The small burning droplets fell like shrapnel onto his waiting skin. Beat by beat, he'd try to bear it as long as he could. Every day, he could tolerate seconds longer than the previous, and every day, he'd lower the temperature until his breathing eased. After the shower, he stood in front of the fogged mirror, turning on the bathroom fan to let out the sauna he created. Droplets of water ran down the painted bathroom walls, collecting in small pools on the floor. No doubt that mold was growing somewhere, but why should he worry about a slow respiratory death when the more immediate and extreme await him every day.

The mirror started clearing and Michael could make out parts of his face. When he gave up on sleeping, he thought of words, phrases, and songs that might bring himself back whole. He reviewed his life, his likes, his loves. There was nothing too trivial, nothing too stupid that wasn't worth trying. He knew one man who used the names of women he'd had sex with. There was another who used the 2001 Patriots starting offensive line. Many parents used their kids' names and many offspring their parents. When Michael liked things, he liked baseball. He liked movies. He can remember these things, yet have no attachment to them in the present, as if he were trapped behind glass and the things he once loved in life were just beyond that thin, invisible barrier.

"Take me out to the ball game, take me out to the crowds. Buy me some peanuts and crackerjacks...", he spoke to the mirror. The whole song, without melody. Even when he did like things, he knew he didn't like singing. He tried a few more phrases and names, but nothing changed. His father liked John Wayne and he'd said about every variation of "Saddle up, Pilgrim" he could think of and they never worked. It had been so long that he wasn't even sure what "turning off" would feel like. He thought that maybe he'd cry. That would be a novel sensation. His face endured a quick shave, then he stepped out of the bathroom and walked over to his mother in her chair. Her hard look was gone for a second and as her eyes met his, the scowl came back and she threw her fury at him. She often waited like that for him, the second of peace more like an invitation to feel that he could not oblige.

"Bout damn time. Some of us would like to use the bathroom today. Inconsiderate, unfeeling machine!" she ranted. "And while we're at it, you don't have to rush me with breakfast, you know. Bad enough you're feeding me this crap. You don't have to shovel it down my throat, too."

Michael had no response. It was routine at this point. She would strike and he defend. She was old and he did dangerous work. It was only a matter of time before they were free of each other.

"Is this any way to live? Sitting on this chair, watching television all day. And at least I have that again. Before might have been harder, but at least I could move around the house. I could go outside and breathe. I'm a prisoner here. Stuck in this tiny rat trap. And my warden isn't even here half the time. I could die right after you leave and you might not notice 'til you come stumbling home drunk like the degenerate you are."

He bent down next to the chair and looked her right in the eyes. He wasn't quite docile but wasn't threatening. Instead, he gave a look that an owner gave an unruly pet or a stern parent to a rebellious child. She looked back, stabbing at him in her pupils. Then, she took a drag of a cigarette and blew the smoke right in his face. Michael turned and coughed and she smiled, content with her victory.

Michael waved his hand to distribute the fumes, then turned and made his way out the door. He'd installed several locks and a steel grate over the main door to keep away anyone who had no qualms about robbing old women. Every day he locked them all and every day he paused, wondering if he could "forget" just this once. He fumbled with the keys in his hand, weighing the options over and over, but as if he were possessed by some higher altruism, he'd always lock the locks, keeping his mother safe from the world that he chose to confront every day. Today was no different, except that it took him longer.

He climbed down the stairs of their pre-war apartment building, passing kicked-in doors, steel doors, plywood doors with spray paint, just like Arlo's neighborhood. When Deluge started clearing buildings, no two blocks would have the same story. Downtown was a disaster. Uptown, abandoned. The business district, burnt to the ground. Neighbors turned on each other like rats escaping a sinking ship. There were two kinds of corpses. The ones that lived long enough to starve to death and the ones that died early, fighting for food, supplies, and anything else of value.

One building stuck out in his mind in particular. A six floor apartment building with the luxury of a metal fence, so Gothic in style, that Michael thought of older cemeteries and cathedrals when the truck rolled up in front. He found it odd that the fence looked like it had just been painted, as small paint globs gathered at the bottom and pooled around each fence post. As the team unloaded, they hadn't yet met resistance. Most people were too weak to function, straining to form smiles as their apparent rescuers had come to save them from starvation. This building, however, looked on the outside like everything was normal. The floors inside were polished. The fixtures dusted. Even the mailboxes were buffed and shiny. Chief, who although polite, was never against kicking in doors, was knocking as if he were trying to sell the occupants a vacuum cleaner or fringe religion.

The first door answered and a smiling, older couple met the recruiters. They looked full-bellied and although gracious hosts, they seemed annoyed with the disturbance. Michael remembered feeling like he'd traveled back in time, to the bygone era of civilized folk, where knocks on the door weren't met with berserkers or the terminally desperate. Michael sat on a couch covered in plastic. The others went to clear the rest of the floor.

"What can we do for you, son?" the man asked.

"We work for Deluge," Chief replied, visibly confused. "We've been going from building to building trying to clear out the dead and bring whoever's still alive back into society."

"Oh, well isn't that lovely. I was just telling Marvin the other day that someone ought to do something about the smell. I can only hold my tongue about it for so long", the woman replied.

"How, if I may ask, were you able to do all of this? I mean, everything outside of this building is gone to hell and this place seems almost pleasant."

"Oh, you'll have our Super, Herman, to thank for that. He's real handy. He lives in the basement and he's been able to keep the building looking good and together, we, I mean the building, we've been able to stick together and tough it out," Marvin replied, putting his hand on his wife's knee.

"Yes, but how? How do you have water?"

"Rain reclamation mostly. Herman converted the boiler and all of the pipes into a sort of cistern that gets refilled when it rains. Usually, we're able to get a bucket a day or so in the basement. Otherwise, some of the younger people would go out and find what they could. Some days are better than others, I admit, but we like to keep positive around here," the woman replied. While neither were fat, they had fat on them. Michael hadn't seen a person with anything other than sinew and skeletons that wished to escape their skin suits. He could only wonder, trying to find the words without offending their still intact sensibilities.

"How have you," he started, "been eating so well?"

They both started laughing. It went on a little longer than Michael thought appropriate, then continued a bit longer. The old man had a tear in his eye. "If you go see Herman, he'll explain everything," the woman said with a smile. They both looked at him with novelty, staring him up and down, and followed him as he left the apartment. The couple stood at the door as Michael turned to say goodbye and they gave him a small wave.

"When you're done with Herman, we can have you and your friends for dinner," and with that, Michael knew that if he went into that basement, he wouldn't be coming out. The team met back up in the foyer after clearing all six floors. Each one was referred to Herman and each apartment was full of smiling faces and stuffed bellies.

"These people are sick," Caroline said.

"It's kind of brilliant," Donahue countered, "Attract outsiders with that nice facade and bring them to the basement to get served for dinner. If I needed to eat people, I'd do it that way."

"Well, of course, you'd do that, Donahue," Gomez replied.

"Wasn't Peterson with you?" Michael asked.

"I thought I sent him to go get you," Chief replied.

Not much time passed as an ear-shattering scream rang out through the building. Michael had been on several battlefields before, hearing men and women die with thousands of explosions providing a steel curtain of sound in the background. This scream, unaccompanied, sounded so strange. It was so clear, like the primeval sound of human agony. Michael thought of Cain and Abel and what hell would sound like if he ever went there. He imagined Peterson's screams would echo from circle to circle on repeat, like a record of suffering, skipping for all eternity.

They found another way to the basement, probably the one the residents used and made a careful descent into the building's dark underbelly. Caroline stayed behind, her rifle at the ready, in case their hosts thought to swarm them. The staircase was in an uncovered courtyard, where all manner of butchers equipment and rotting pieces of human meat were sitting in the open. Leftover scalps were piled in a corner, at least a hundred, if not more. There was another corner for bones, though even the most civilized person could imagine uses for leftover bones, so there weren't as many piled up. The concrete ground had scratch marks in it, some gone over enough times to make tiny grooves.

The laundry room door at the other end of the courtyard had a deadbolt on it and was splattered in a dark red that was instinctively recognizable as blood. Some time back in human evolution, an ancestor developed an immediate reaction towards blood that even Michael, with his cybernetics and emotional suppressants, couldn't help but succumb to. All the while, Peterson's screams continued, until they didn't. Michael could have sworn he'd heard him saying his words, in a vain attempt at stopping his pain.

They opened the deadbolt and inside were the apartment's living cattle, who subsided on the meat of their once fellow captives. They were each chained to a corner of the room, unable to move and try to end their suffering prematurely. Their naked skin was pale, almost albino. One man was missing both arms below the elbow, wearing a matching set of tourniquets a few inches above wounds. A woman had the same treatment to a leg. There was no fear in them, only waiting. Michael had seen starving people try to kiss his feet and hail him a rescuer. He'd seen angry mobs of hoarders try to shoe him away. But only then, in the faces of those who were waiting to be eaten, did he see people who were living against their will and were moaning and gasping for swift permanence. There were four and when Michael finished firing, there were none. And then they went to see Herman.

Another door led to the building maintenance apparatus. The boiler, the trash, and a small workshop for the super were all behind this door. Chief kicked it in, only to find a short, balding man covered in a thick plastic apron and wearing a clear visor over his face. In one hand, he held a dull handsaw and the other, he raised in an attempt to surrender. Peterson was dead. When they'd seen that, Chief did not hesitate to dispatch the superintendent on the spot.

"What do we do now?" Gomez asked.

"We round up the people and bring them into the fold. Same old," Donahue answered.

47

"How the fuck do we explain a bunch of cannibals? No one is going to trust them and they might end up preferring human flesh to anything else," Gomez persuaded.

"These aren't people anymore. There are rules," Chief answered. "Basic fucking rules. They had no problem looking us in the eyes as if we were going to be on the menu a little later. If our mission is to bring civilization back, then these… things have no place in the future we want to build." He spoke in a calm, quiet fury and was greeted with nods in agreement.

Gomez and Donahue went to guard the fire escapes. No doubt they'd try to run once they heard the gunshots. Meanwhile, the polite knocking went the way of the dodo and each apartment door was met with a boot or the battering ram. Michael led the charge against the old couple and he saw the fear in their eyes. He was used to that look. He understood that look. It was a mix of surprise and desperation. Michael wondered if the old woman would hide behind her husband or maybe the coward would throw his wife at him, but neither happened. They stood together, hand in hand, and dropped less than a second apart, their blood mixing together in a neat pool below them.

The rest of the building was more of the same. More scared, shocked looks. More bodies. More spilled blood. Took them another couple of hours before all was said and done and when the clean-up crew got there, Michael could see no look of horror on their faces through the HAZMAT suits. Instead, they regarded it as routine. In the debriefing, Captain Marcus looked furious as he read the after-action report. Michael and the others could only sit and be dressed down.

"Cowboys! You're a bunch of undisciplined, goddamned Cowboys! You get orders to do a routine sweep and turn it into some fucking murder house."

"Sir, we felt- I felt, that it would be difficult to integrate these people back into society. The level of mania that most of them were operating at wa-"

"Ain't shit compared to what some of the other teams have found. You better harden the fuck up, Axel. You and your whole team better put on your big boy pants and do your goddamn jobs. We haven't even tried going to Manhattan and you want to pull this shit on me. Scouting report has that fucking place on another goddamn level. Race wars. Gang wars. People crucified from goddamn traffic lights. Not sure where they got all the rifles, but they have a shit load of them, and once they have someone else to point them at besides each other, it's going to be real bloody."

He took a moment to collect himself.

"I can't have this again, do we have an understanding?"

"Yes, Sir," they replied, sporadically.

"I'm docking your pay for this mess. Sixty-Six bodies at fifty D-Coin a pop. Be lucky it isn't more because I know most of them were able-bodied."

Michael thought about the four in the laundry room. The looks on their faces. Their bodies were just as plump as the building inhabitants but were in no way able-bodied. Michael often saw their faces and thought of all the faces of those who

49

were living against their will. And he thought himself fortunate. The old woman could go to hell, but he'd keep locking the door.

CHAPTER FOUR

Purple zone detail was a welcome duty, rotated between the teams every few weeks. Michael appreciated the quiet. He liked the green zone, too, but was a minority. Word from on high was that people in the Green Zone were to be left alone. No money to be made there. Just outside, in the Purp, you could get a few people to come willingly, make a few bucks that way or make enough through other types of incentive. Since Arlo's, they'd been on purple patrol for a week and they knew the good times were coming to a close.

Michael took Newbie and Donahue down a block of recently re-homed refugees, knocking on doors, checking off lists, and turning a blind eye to anything that wasn't considered their business. There was screaming in the whore-houses, shots fired in the gambling dens, and explosions from the meth labs that stacked in between.

They strolled into Diamond Jake's jewelry store, darting right to his office in the back, located in the heart of the Purp. He was a large man, well built, and although on the fatter side, still formidable. His age showed in his thinning white hair and hanging jowls, which drooped off his chin, sinking onto his broad chest. He had a grit in his eye that seemed more a cause

51

of his survival than an effect of May Day. All kinds of artwork, salvaged and looted from all around, surrounded them. Tiny gaps of white paint came through between the works that otherwise smothered the walls. There were only two chairs, but no one sat, instead, spreading themselves out along the room. Donahue stuck to the corner near the door, while Newbie distracted himself with the art. Only Michael met Jake head on and shook hands.

"Good to see you. Whose this new Golem you've brought to me today?" His thick Russian, Yiddish accent announced. It was deep, firm, and did not betray Jake's intentions. He was a businessman, through and through.

"That's Newbie, Jake", Michael answered. "You see him, you think of me, okay?"

"Only you are you. The other Golems need a firmer hand", he said, mashing his fist into his catcher's mitt sized palm, ready for Michael's pitch.

"How's business?"

"Steady. I never take on more than I can chew."

"Seems like you can chew a lot, Jakey", Donahue butted in. A wave of indifference passed over Jake's face as he addressed Donahue.

"That's a warning. I don't like rudeness. Tell him what I do to rude people", he said, not looking away from Donahue.

Donahue knew Jake's reputation. He'd worked enough of these jobs. Jewish men were not stereotyped as brutal enforcers. They'd been called every name and slur in the book, but intimidating was not one of them. Yet, Jake seemed to break all molds and stared down Donahue until he broke the gaze and submitted himself by darting his eyes to the floor. The warmth came back as he turned his attention back over to Michael, who nodded, hoping that all was copacetic again.

"You Golems leave", he commanded Newbie and Donahue. "I talk to this one alone now".

"What you've got to say to him, you can say to us, Jake. Newbie's good or else he wouldn't be here, capisce?" Donahue replied.

"New Golem is least of my worries. I talk to you", he looked at Michael. "Two others wait in store. Talk to Chaim. He give you both new watches. Gift of understanding, yes?"

That turned Donahue's attitude around as a smile came to his face and he grabbed Newbie, who hadn't had time to react to the news. "Alright, Jakey, you're the boss. Won't see us messing with your little pow-wow, no sir. Come on, Newbie, let's teach you a thing or two about style, eh?"

The door shut and Jake relaxed his shoulders, then stood and gave Michael a bear hug.

"Mishka, I've been getting worried. It's been too long."

"Only been a couple months."

53

"Is lifetime these days. How's your mother?"

"Alive."

"Best can be hoped for. And I am good, too, boychik, thanks so much for asking."

"Why ask when I can see you. Plus, I knew you were going to tell me."

"You're too much like Golem, Mishka. Is no good. Always have serious face. My Rosa used to say, 'Mishka has very serious face', right before you make mess in your diaper. You don't remember, you were little baby. But you have same face right now, but I don't think bowel movement would help."

"How's the old house?"

"Still there. I have my boys stick around. They're good, won't go doing anything not supposed to".

His mother complained about the house, but Michael never told her he'd made assurances to keep it intact. He planned on surprising her one day when it was safe to move back in, but enough time had passed that it looked less and less possible. That and her constant whining made him resent ever trying to do her any favors.

"That other Golem is too rude. Come into my store and make jokes. Bet he would not like I make joke about him."

"Bet you're right."

"Mishka, you need to be looking out for that one. He has trouble writing on his face."

If Jake only knew. "I've got it handled."

"You ask me and I do what is necessary. Anything for you, Boychik, you know this. Since little boy, I tell you this and you never ask. You were good boy. All other neighborhood children were loud and too much. You and Daisy, good children. My Rosa loved you like our own. Your parents were good neighbors. I always remember your father mowing lawn when my knees went bad. Never complain. I never forget him. Just as you never forget Baba Rosa, eh?"

"Never."

He wiped a few tears and smiled. "Excuse me. Too much sad talk for business meeting. You come over for dinner and we talk like old times. Then, I can cry. Never at office. Such things make me look weak. So, I hear rumors that New York push coming soon, yes?"

Michael wasn't surprised that Jake knew something was up. His wife was a notorious gossip growing up. If the military had invested in turning town gossips into informants, Michael was sure that they would never have lost a single war. But femininity was anathema to war, especially American War. Jake, who'd been surviving her loss for almost ten years at this point, picked up several tools of the trade, and being a jeweler, must have heard his own share of secrets from the clients who congregated around his display cases.

"I get my intel from you. They don't tell us anything until it's too late."

"They're going to Manhattan in two weeks. From what I've been told, it is not a pleasant place to be. But, there is already one section of the city that is yours, if the rules are followed, that is."

Michael sat and listened, expressing interest, though he already knew what Jake was going to say.

"My people are tough, but they shouldn't have to fight any wars."

"Everyone's gotta do their part, Jake."

"I do their part for them, then, yes?"

"You're in contact with a Jewish community in Manhattan?"

"Is surprise? Thousands of Jews live in Manhattan."

"Not sure how many people are left in Manhattan."

"When you cross GW, you'll be near Yeshiva University. There, you will find safe place to start from. Is good. Just don't take my people, Mishka, please."

"How can I say no, Jake. You've been like a father to me."

"No. I am only old neighbor. You only have one father, Mishka. Remember him."

Michael got up to leave and tried to shake Jake's hand, but he pulled him in tight for a hug. Michael, unused to the physical affection, patted the old man's back a few times before being released.

"Watch that you do not become Golem, Mishka. There is still hope for you, Boychik."

"I'm alright, Jake. Promise."

Michael left for the door and got his fingers around the knob when Jake called back. "Wait! I almost forget. I have job for you and your friends. Talk to Chaim and he give you instructions. Some people think they can get my protection without paying their own way. Many young, healthy men trying to hide from the Golems. They're all yours if you bring me that cocksucker, Barnes. You'll know him when you see him. He's asshole schmuck. Only one with suit and haircut."

Michael took Donahue and Newbie to the edge of the Purp, where Tyler Barnes was holding up. They called in the rest of the team and a truck for backup, but had them stay back. It was easier to catch them off guard and recruiting trucks stuck out and a lot of locals knew which teams were coming by the markings on their vehicles. Michael's team were known as cowboys, though much of their reputation came from Donahue's antics.

It was an old tenement building, pre-war, in slum conditions. The roof looked caved in on one end, but it was still better than a good portion of spots in the purp. There was a guard outside, but the only threat he posed was that he was tall, lean, and could probably call for help. His shaved head and tattooed knuckles indicated he could handle most trouble that came through but was probably a coward in all other aspects. They'd soon find out and Michael let Newbie take the lead. The training wheels needed to come off at some point.

"We're looking for Barnes", Newbie demanded.

"Sorry, friend. Don't know him", replied the guard.

"We'll take a look around for him, just to be sure", Donahue replied, patting the man on the shoulder. The guard's eyes darted and before he could call out for help, Michael hit him in the head with the butt of his rifle.

"Tie him up", Michael commanded Newbie, who dragged him inside and tied him to a radiator in the tenement's lobby with some flex-cuffs. Michael called in the others and the trucks rolled up. There were more than a few runners, always were. Maybe one or two got away, but they'd get caught one day. Or not. It was what it was and Michael was content with the haul he had, rather than the crumbs he did not.

Barnes was easy enough to spot. His burgundy suit was pressed, clean, and he made no attempt to hide when Michael called out to him. Michael and Donahue cleared rooms, while Newbie covered them. They made it into one room and found a young woman, naked, and tied to an old bed, with a fearful look in her eye. Donahue went in first, if not drooling, then close to it.

"Never look a gift horse in the mouth eh, boys", he told them. Michael turned around and Newbie shuddered. Donahue closed the door and there was a loud commotion and six gunshots, followed by shouting and cursing.

"Fucking sneaky fuck", Donahue shouted as Michael kicked the door in. Donahue was standing over a man in his underwear with three bullet holes in his chest. The girl was also shot in the head and her brains decorated the headboard behind her, her tied arms and legs limp. Newbie muttered a prayer and crossed himself, while Donahue kept cursing at the dead bodies.

"Motherfucker was in the closet. My pants are halfway down when he jumps me and busts my fucking watch. I just got this thing" he said, showing the broken timepiece hanging off his wrist, the face smashed and a gear sticking out. "And he made me shoot the fucking girl. Wonder if it's still warm", he laughed.

Chief called in on the radio and Michael gave him the all-clear. Donahue searched the dead man and found his clothes in the corner. There was a gold wedding band on his left hand, which Donahue pillaged.

"Stupid fuck", he muttered, loosening the ring off the finger.

The trucks were loaded up, twenty-two in all minus the two Donahue shot. A great haul for Purple duty. Michael, Donahue, and Newbie walked Barnes back to Jake's store. Chief gave them a nod as he drove away. When they got there, Jake was standing outside, surrounded by a few of his men and tens of onlookers. The kind man he knew growing up was replaced by an executioner, whose grimace both impressed and surprised Michael. As they walked Barnes in, Michael heard Donahue probing the prisoner.

"Nice shoes. What size are they?"

"My size."

"Nice watch, too. How's about it, eh? Not like you can take it with you."

"Fuck off, Rep."

"Suit yourself. One way or another, I'll have it. Just was hoping I didn't need to clean blood off of it."

They reached Jake and Barnes was pushed into the dirt, his fine suit now covered in a thick layer of dirt.

"Hiya, Jake", Barnes greeted. "Well, no need to fling any bullshit. I tried to fuck you. I knew what might happen, but I figured 'Hey, maybe it'll work'. Just know, I meant no disrespect."

Jake said nothing, instead just giving a slight nod.

"I'd prefer it didn't hurt too much."

The crowd grew restless at the chatter, though nothing above whispers. Men and women were rocking side to side and back and forth, anxious to see what would happen next. Newbie nudged Michael. "What are all these people doing here?"

"This is their Super Bowl. Now shut up and look dangerous."

One of Jake's men walked over with a long, rusty machete. There were notches in the blade, so many, that it looked serrated. The intact parts looked dull like they could not even pop a balloon. It was stained with blood in the rusted parts and the wooden handle. Barnes' eyes darted between the machete and Jake and a small dampness formed along his brow and ran down the side of his face.

"Hope you're strong, Jake. Would hate to feel it. And maybe they see you not kill me in one shot, eh? Maybe they see you're getting old. Better to shoot me and have them wonder than tried to cut off my fucking head and prove you're not as spry as you once were", Barnes reasoned.

Jake contemplated for a moment before winding up to swing, his mid-section torquing around and slingshotting around, the blade moving forward with great speed, making contact with Barnes' neck and slicing through as if there were no resistance at all. If Jake were weak, he didn't show it now. Michael saw the crowd start to dissipate, murmurs of satisfaction echoing as they went their separate ways. Donahue ran over to the headless corpse and snagged the watch off of Barnes' wrist, blood still spurting out of the neck and deepening the red of the fine burgundy suit. Jake's men went to stop him, but Jake waved them off.

"Golem can take", he said, turning back to his store. As he entered, he kept the open sign facing forward, a signal that he and Michael had come up with a few years ago. Michael was invited to dinner. It had been a few months, if not more, since the last time. The old man would reminisce about the old days, about his wife, about his sins. Michael got to enjoy real food and a longer reprieve from the war at home. Michael went back to the station, filled out some paperwork on the recruits, and headed back to the Purp incognito.

Jake had always been an excellent cook. Even when the grocery stores were full, he insisted on cooking the parts of animals that no one ever ate. Tongue, tripe, brain, he made them all delicious. When most children his age had trouble eating their vegetables, Michael shoveled an Eastern European version of Haggis, whose name he'd forgotten, but whose memory was stamped in his olfactory bulb. This, still, was gourmet to him and Michael looked forward to a nice, warm meal.

There was real silverware, freshly polished, sitting on the table when Michael took his seat. It was the set he'd used as a boy and was in pristine condition. The plates were fine china, though Michael could not discern where they'd come from, nor if their quality were even that luxurious. It would surprise him if he found out they were knock-offs or from Ikea. Jake and Rosa always had nice things. 'Why pay many times over for what you can pay for once?' he always asked young Michael. Beef liver and onions were on the menu and Michael ate his fill, his host quiet until Michael had eaten about half of his portion. Though Michael seldom used flowery language, the word exquisite came to mind.

"You like, Boychik?"

"It is very good, yes. Thank you."

"Ach, you don't thank family. Especially the family you choose."

Michael saw the warmth and love in Jake's eyes. He looked on Michael as if he were still the young boy who'd sat at that same table with the same fork and knife, and whose table manners were less than refined, but showed a level of effort reserved only for those one loved and respected. Michael couldn't find a salad fork and would use a dessert spoon for his soups, but he never put his elbows on the table, ate with intention and care for the meal, as well as its chef, and used the napkin with the daintiness of the most proper gentlemen. The look in Jake's eyes made it difficult for him to understand how his host and the man who chopped off Barnes' head were one and the same. Michael was at this point, immune to horror, but Jake's actions more confused him than repulsed him. He wondered how Jake could be so complex, when he, the unfeeling machine, was so simple.

"What did he do? Barnes, I mean. He said he tried to fuck you. How?"

"Nothing that warranted what I did to him. It's a new world, Mishka. One where cruelty rules the day."

Michael felt the comment was obvious. Jake knew what he'd become, yet still treated Michael like the child he helped to raise.

"It is what it is, Jake."

"Not that simple. Do you know what killing Tyler Barnes did for me today? It bought me a couple of weeks of peace, maybe even a month. Those people who watched will tell others and they'll fear me. My men will see that I'm worth following. It might not have looked like it, but I was surprised that his head

63

came off so clean. I thought for sure that I was too old to get that much force. I'd have blamed a dull blade and people would have accepted that for a short while, but now, I am still one to be feared. Now the streets can still be safe. Now women don't get raped, except by Golems, who I can't touch. No murders either, unless I command it."

Jake often poured a glass of wine with dinner, but Michael never saw him touch it in the years he'd known the old man. Tonight, he took liberal sips of the glass and even poured a second and third as the night went on.

"How many people have you killed, Michael?"

"Seventy-three."

"Seventy-three", he muttered, shaking his head. He said something in Yiddish that Michael couldn't understand. "I've killed Sixteen, including Barnes today. The first one was during the lockdown. A kid. Teenager broke in and was looking for something he could sell. I smacked him with a baseball bat and he broke his neck on the coffee table. His eyes were still open. I always thought they closed like in the movies. And they were blank. I was waiting for him to stare at me, guilt me with his dead gaze, but it wasn't like that either. How many people do you think you saved by killing?"

There were tears on the old man's face, tucking in between the wrinkles. Michael knew he'd never saved another life from killing, not even before the ETP.

"I've sent over three hundred Jews over to Israel since taking over Purple zone. My men are Jews, too. Israeli Defense Force.

They don't follow me. Not really. They're on a mission. I get too old or too weak, they find someone else to accomplish mission. I'm on the same mission, Mishka. Maybe that will be my salvation. That I killed Sixteen, but saved many more, right? Right?"

"That's right, Jake", he replied and the old man smiled, but Michael lied. There was no salvation, especially for killers. And Michael paid for his sins every day.

They ended dinner and Jake went to give Michael a hug, which Michael returned with a simple wrap around the shoulders. The old, bear of a man, sunk his head into Michael's shoulder and started sobbing, squeezing Michael tight to him.

"My Rosa is gone. Your father is gone. Your sister. You and your mama are all I have. And you're both so different. You're more Golem than man, Mishka. I pretend it's not true, but I know. I'm all alone now."

He let Michael go and Michael headed for the door, unable to console the old man. As he left, he saw two of Jake's men looking at one another as sobs from inside could still be heard. They were laughing and although Michael couldn't understand what they were saying, he was not so naive to think it wasn't about Jake. He stepped past them and as fast as he could, removed the sidearm from one of the soldier's holsters. He whipped the young man, who couldn't have been older than Seventeen and brought him to his knees. His partner tried to draw his weapon but fumbled with the rifle as Michael drew down on him.

"You didn't hear or see anything. Nod if you understand."
They nodded.

He let the young soldier go and dropped the pistol into the
dirt, then headed home as if nothing had happened. He couldn't
console the old man, but he could protect him.

CHAPTER FIVE

There was a fluttering of chatter in the briefing room. Michael did not doubt that more "routine sweeps" were on the agenda, but there was a nervous energy in the room that didn't match that occasion. He was already missing the Purp. Whispers and murmurs about a breakout in the south created rumors of large bounties and long trips away from home, where the per diem pay would make even the most fruitless expeditions worthwhile. Michael sat with his team, who themselves could not help but be consumed by the gossip and the titillating mystery that hung in the air. Captain Marcus came to the podium at the front of the room, flanked by a couple of stuffed suits.

"Alright, alright," he started, but the murmurs kept up, "Shut up, damn it!" and silence followed. The Captain had sweat stains under his armpits and small beads formed on top of his shaved head, running down his face and all meeting at his chin. The Captain, like the rest of them, was a soldier, a member of the old guard. His body language was reserved, almost trying to hide behind the podium, where most days, it seemed like he wanted to get the thing out of his way, gripping it tight and almost throwing it across the room so the recruiters could get a better look at him. The two suits were average-looking white men, wore sunglasses indoors, and possessed almost no discernible features except that one had brown hair and the other, jet black.

"Today, we're making a push with the newly formed Third Army into Manhattan. This has been a long time coming and Corporate finally has enough manpower to start clearing the city. They've secured the GW and made a foothold across into Washington Heights. The West Side Highway is littered with cars, bumper to bumper, so the main push down south will be like a goddamn monster truck rally. Tanks will clear the way, pushing through what they can and crushing everything else. We won't be going in until the Third has cleared the streets."

A large Map was projected onto the wall and although it had all kinds of bells and whistles, the Captain wasn't the kind for panache and spectacle. He grabbed several dry erase markers and drew arrows on the projection screen to make his point.

"It'll be a piecemeal operation, starting North and coming back around, then a general push South. Intel suggests that Washington Heights will be the easiest to pacify and that it'll get a lot harder once the streets get narrower. That's all I've got for now, any questions?"

Every hand shot up in the air. Five minutes of questions and answers only grated the Captain's already thinning nerve before he finally boiled over. "Listen! You'll get more information when you get your assignments. Section leaders, get to the trucks. Pack your rucks, this won't be a day trip." One of the suits whispered something in the Captain's ear as the recruiters jostled out of their seats. "Oh, one more thing. Connors. Donahue. In my office. You're going on special assignment."

Michael was surprised at the announcement. He never thought himself outstanding in any kind of way. He tried not to be. He figured he could keep his head down and do his job until the time that he could find work that didn't involve incoming fire. And to be on special assignment with Donahue was no prize, either. The man was certifiable. Any duty that involved him was going to get tangled, complicated, and worst of all, bloodied.

"Hear that Gomez? I've got a special mission," Donahue chided. "Good luck getting your head chopped off across the river."

"Chief, what do we do down two men?" Caroline asked. "It's hard enough clearing buildings with six, but four? Good luck."

"I'll talk to the Captain when we get there. Now doesn't seem like the time."

"I've never seen him like that," Newbie replied.

"You two better get to his office," Chief added. "And don't do anything stupid that would piss him off. Shit rolls downhill."

Michael and Donahue walked out of the briefing room, down a wide hall that led to the Captain's office. As they approached, yelling could be heard from inside.

"You have no idea what you are asking of us!" Michael heard. The sound was muffled by the thick door and cement walls, but the Captain seemed able to break through those obstructions. The other two were quiet, and although Michael was curious, he wasn't about to put his ear up to the door. Donahue was less interested and knocked on the door, ending the argument inside.

"Enter," Captain Marcus declared, having yet to adjust his volume. The two entered and the Captain seemed relieved that they were there.

"Connors, Donahue, these men work for corporate. It seems that Alex Mercer has asked for you both specifically, so you'll be missing out on the fun ahead. I expect you to do your jobs and uphold the standards we have here. They're all yours." Michael was unsure who that last line was meant for.

They piled into an old, black Cadillac Escalade. Michael noticed it had run-flat tires and when the door swung open, he saw a thick, steel frame. The tinted windows were at least a half-inch thick and below the interior door handle was a small first aid kit. He thought about the truck they rolled in and how it was almost twice the size of this SUV, but if there were any trouble, Michael would choose the Caddy. All Donahue noticed were the leather seats and mini-bar. He was a happy camper, with a whiskey sour in one hand and a vodka soda in the other. One tight turn ruined all of that though, and the drinks landed on his uniform, an act of cosmic Karma that made Michael question his atheism.

The truck pulled into the green zone, a semi-walled off section of the Jersey City peninsula that started where the Lincoln Tunnel used to funnel in commuters to New York, Deluge managed to keep mostly intact from the beginning of the whole mess by taking control of all the ports and shipping in supplies and food. People can say a lot about Alex Mercer, but they can't call him a coward. When the rest of the world was running for their lives and everyone who could afford it was making a mass exodus, Alex Mercer stayed and tried to save the sinking ship. And in the opinion of most, he was doing it, too. When Michael was first hired by Deluge, he was like a cop, bringing order to the lawless streets. He thought of himself as Wyatt Earp or Bat Masterson or even Pat Garrett, though his father had always thought of Garrett as a traitor and taught Michael at a young age to consider betrayal worse than any other sin. How strange it is, what the brain decides to keep as important.

Michael didn't think much about his father or his sister for that matter. His mother never brought them up either and he only saw her as the annoying, haggish crone that ate, slept, and slowly killed herself on the lazy boy in the living room. When he left to join the Army, Jersey City was up and coming. When he came back, it had up and come, due in no small part to Alex Mercer and Deluge. When the world went to shit, Deluge tried to hold on to as much as it could and if they could make the rest of the world even a fraction as pleasant as the Green Zone, then Michael felt duty-bound to be part of it. It was something deeper than emotion. Something not even his fucked up brain could filter out. That it paid well was only a bonus.

Children were playing on the streets. The grocery store they passed was full of fruits and vegetables and even a few choice cuts of meat advertised in the windows. The streets were clean and newly paved. Michael almost thought it ridiculous to be riding in that luxury tank until he heard a loud explosion from across the river. The offensive had started and Michael was pulled back to the real world just as the SUV pulled up in front of the Olympus Building.

When he'd seen it as a kid, he remembered the marble columns. His father worked in a building nearby that was all glass and steel and was the architectural equivalent of tapioca pudding. He remembered the days his father would bring him to work and he'd sneak out to go look at the Olympus Building, which towered high above all the others in Jersey City and even blocked out some of New York's skyline. As he walked through its large, ornate doors, Michael thought about how a younger him would be more excited.

Walking through the lobby, Michael took note of the lines of columns that guided visitors to a grand fountain in the middle, with a copy of the Venus de Milo, this time with arms, fixed atop. No doubt it was all real marble, but Michael was only thinking of which one would provide the best cover in case the violence of the world penetrated this palace. Donahue meanwhile was acting like a tourist, pointing at the classic pieces of art that were "rescued" from across the river and Michael was thankful that the buffoon didn't have a camera.

They rode up a private elevator to the top floor. Together they exited into a narrow corridor, with all litany of doors flanked to their right and left, much in the same way their two escorts were. Each door had a gold name placard with words like "War Room", "Meeting Room", "Residence", and a whole list of others. Most had joked that Alex Mercer crowned himself President of the United States and from the grandiose sense that the Olympus Building gave off, there was little doubt he thought so himself. Through the main door at the end of the hall was led to a waiting room next to Mercer's private secretary.

She was a good looking woman by most standards, but one of the features of Michael's extended emotional exile was the lack of a sex drive. No such absences existed in Donahue, however, and he walked his way over to her, leaning over the desk to talk. In what seemed like only minutes later, he was whispering in her ear and Michael could hear soft giggles and smiles come from her soft, dainty face. "If she only knew", Michael thought, wanting to shake his head.

There was a call to let Donahue in and, being Donahue, he swaggered his way into Mercer's office as the secretary followed and shut the door behind him. He was in there only ten minutes and when he came out, he was wearing a toothful smile. "Payday, Mike. Payday," was all he said as he got the secretary's info and walked back toward the elevator. Mercer's voice from inside the office called to Michael, and Michael felt like he'd entered a Dragon's lair.

The spacious office dwarfed everything around it and gave a view of New York reserved for airplanes and birds of prey. There was a large sitting area and a great oak desk in front of the windows. There was no one else in the room, at least no one Michael could see, except for him and Mercer. Mercer wasn't particularly tall, but not short either. Probably around five foot ten. He had light olive skin that looked of a healthy tan and wore a fine silk suit with gray pinstripes. He was standing in front of the grand window, looking across as small fireballs flew into the air where the Army, and Michael's team, were doing their jobs and bringing New York back to civilization.

"So, Mike Connors. At last. I wonder, what are you thinking right now? Did you ever think you'd ever be in the same room as me?"

"Honestly?"

"Of Course," he said, sipping his drink. It looked like whiskey. Probably even scotch. He could afford it.

"Honestly, probably the same way Dorthy felt when the Wizard turned out to be an old man."

That made him spit out his drink and laugh. Michael wondered how much that laugh cost.

"I've never seen that movie."

"Me neither. It's just one of those things. Everyone knows about it."

"I like you. More than that other guy. The whole time, he was kissing my ass. Calling me Mr. Mercer. But there was this thing in his eye, like if at any moment he'd just snap and rip my goddamn head off."

Michael gave him points for seeing through Donahue's bullshit.

"It makes me wonder why you haven't done anything about it," Mercer added.

"What do you mean?"

"I've read both of your personnel files. Your section leader has nothing but praise for you. Mr. Donahue on the other hand, well let's see," he started thumbing through a manila folder on his desk, "Aggressive battery against some recruits. Sexual misconduct. He even bit off another Recruiter's ear like he's

Mike Tyson or something. So I wonder why none of you ever put that mad dog out of his misery? Loyalty? Fear?"

Michael thought about it. It was something he thought about a lot. Donahue was every bit the monster that Mercer described. He'd seen it up close. There were opportunities to do it. Times when everyone would have just looked the other way and understood. There were other times when someone else almost did it and Michael would have turned his back and understood. But it is difficult to kill a man who has saved your life, even if you hate him. And Donahue saved the lives of every single one of his teammates at least once. He was the only one they were all sure would live forever, even if it was just because Satan didn't need the competition.

"Same reason as you. A mad dog can be useful when you need something done."

That made Mercer smile and he walked over to Michael, setting his drink down on his desk.

"I want to show you something. Follow me."

They walked back outside to the elevator bank and went down the first hundred floors flew by and so did the next hundred and the two hundred after that. Michael stopped looking at the screen that counted down until the lobby flashed by and he could see that that they still had further to go. The elevator slowed now and after another minute, the screen flashed "B-30" in an ominous red that reminded Michael of old digital clocks.

"Seems like we're halfway to China, eh?" Mercer joked.

Michael nodded.

"I'm used to people thinking my jokes are funny."

"I thought you didn't want a kiss ass." Whether the joke was funny or not wasn't the issue. Norm MacDonald could do his best Thirty and Michael wouldn't crack a smile. It was just the way it was.

"You know why we had to go so deep?"

"No."

"My father based this building off of an Oak tree in front of the house he grew up in. That tree was older than the house. Older than the town he grew up in. When he decided to tear the house down, he uprooted the old tree and saw that the roots were just as deep as the tree was tall. That is the way you build. You go deep to grow tall."

"Or you want to hide something where no one will see it."

Mercer looked at him for a moment, with anger and the hints of fear. Michael gave no response save for his trademark blank stare and Mercer smiled again, leading him out of the elevator.

The lights were off on the whole floor and Mercer found the switch to reveal a sterile, white lab with all kinds of science fiction type creations and gadgets. Half-built robots gathered dust in corners. Experimental weapons lay disassembled on tables next to rolled up blueprints. There was even a Three-D printer about eight feet by ten feet and another ten feet high or so. Mercer passed all of these curiosities to go to a small office within the lab. As they approached the glass door, Michael had noticed that there was a space where a name placard once lived, now removed and the remains scratched away. Mercer opened the door and flipped on the light inside. It was a modest office, nothing like Mercer's. It looked quaint, unassuming, and probably belonged to a character of much the same temperament.

"Hello, THEO,"

"Hello, Alex. Hello Mr. Connors," said a voice that emitted from a speaker on top of the desk."

Michael was put off but did his best to remain calm and at ease. It didn't work.

"Don't worry. I felt the same way when I first started talking to THEO. But, over time, he's become the closest thing I have to a friend. You wanted to see behind the curtain, well Dorthy, meet the Wizard of Deluge International."

"It is nice to meet you, Mr. Connors. I have learned much about you. You are quite adept at your role of recruiting. Probably due to your effectiveness as a soldier beforehand. Would you say that your ETPs have allowed you to take human life much easier and allowed for you to unburden yourself from the psychological trauma that comes with witnessing human suffering?"

Michael didn't have any sort of response. At least, not one off the top of his head.

"You'll have to forgive him, he knows almost everything except manners."

"It's fine."

"THEO, now that you're done insulting our guest, why don't you take the honors and tell him what he's here for."

"Michael Connors has a unique psychological profile, coupled with an advanced level of skill in both the arenas of combat as well as the tracking of human movement and patterns. It is this combination that makes him a rare specimen. One able enough to undergo the necessary mission of finding and terminating the traitor. His combat tours in Persia resulted in a permanent activated state, alleviating him from the emotional weight that comes from prolonged exposure to combat stress, thus creating what Psychologists refer to as 'Miles Automaton'. The Machine Soldier.

Michael winced at the phrasing. He'd heard it many times before from doctors and caseworkers after he'd come home. But this was the first time he'd ever heard it as a compliment. The speaker on the desk had no face, his words were flat as if read from a speak and spell. But Michael heard it. He was sure he heard THEO's approval. That THEO thought of them as the same dwarfed Michael's other foreboding fears about the computer. How did he know so much? When did he create a psychological profile? Why did he think Donahue was suited for the same mission?

"THEO is referring to my former business partner and his creator, Sidney Posner", Mercer cut in. "Sid was- is one of the smartest men on the planet. THEO is his life's work. We started our business together based on his brains and my... I guess we could call it industrial brawn."

"Others might call it money," THEO jabbed.

"I didn't know they could be funny," Michael said, bewildered.

"Yeah, Ol' Sid had his quirks. One was making THEO able to make quips and sarcastic jabs."

"I'm also house-trained," THEO added.

"Is it alive?"

"He is. He woke up just after all this happened, isn't that right, THEO?"

"Correct."

"Why show me any of this?"

"The profile calculated you'd require proof. Donahue is more pragmatic. He named a price, I met it. But you, underneath the government fuck ups, you're a boy scout. Do the right thing for the right reasons. Be all you can be. All that propaganda. You're a goddamn hero."

"You don't expect me to tell anyone about him?"

"Who'd you tell? Who'd believe you? Sidney Posner is the most dangerous man in the country. Probably even the whole world. Everything you see around you. All this death. All this Chaos. All this… Hell, is because of Sidney Posner."

"I believe you may have to qualify those remarks, Alex", THEO added. "That is quite a claim to those who are without the pertinent information."

"Eleven or so years ago, Sidney had a nervous breakdown. He stormed into my office, told me to go to hell, and said he was taking THEO and making his own company. Now, besides the Encyclopedia's worth of case precedent, the multiple NDA's and non-compete contracts, and the miles of code added onto THEO's original framework by Deluge employees, I wouldn't be a good businessman if I let my co-founder leave with the thing that made me the modern Thomas Edison. I tried to talk him off the ledge, but he wouldn't hear it. Then, before he turned into a ghost in the wind, he hacked into the top five biggest banks in the world, withdrew around ten trillion dollars and then just deleted it. Poof. Gone forever. When I'd heard it, I didn't even believe it was possible, but it was and it happened. Then, everyone and their mother ran on the banks, the global economy stalled, crashed, and burned, and those damn Commies on the West Coast made their move. They found the necessary power stations on the East Coast and the Mid-West and blew them up, sending most of the country back to the dark ages."

Michael sat down to take it all in. He figured there were things that Mercer wasn't telling him. No story is that cut and dry. No real story anyway. It's too convenient. Mad Scientist. Its cliche.

"You don't believe me. I get it. It's unbelievable. I wouldn't believe either, except I lived it. For all his faults, Sid was an optimist. I'm sure he thought that when he did what he did, it wouldn't cause the end of days. But you and I are different. We see the people for who they really are. I've long suspected that something like this would happen. Even when you're a Trillionaire, governments don't listen. You tell them about weaknesses. You tell them how to fix them. You even tell them that you'll do it at no cost. Doesn't matter. Too many committees. Too much red tape. Too many hands needing to get greased. I'm a Trillionaire, but I can't print the stuff. Well, at least, I couldn't then. So I decided to just prepare myself. Then, when the leviathan breaks down, people turn to those who have the means and the will to build it back up."

"What do I have to do with this? You want me to go looking for this Posner guy and kill him?"

"Correct," THEO replied in his unsettling tone, "He has recently been spotted by one of our spies inside the PSR. You and Mr. Donahue will travel to San Francisco and meet with him, then you will both dispatch Mr. Posner and return here for your bounty."

The way THEO put it, so neat and simple as if he were asking them to go across the street to borrow a cup of sugar.

"You don't know what you're asking. It would take two armies to get across the country, let alone two men. Why don't you get the goons you've got tailing him to take care of him if they already know where he is?"

"Just as THEO has calculated that you and Mr. Donahue would be the best operatives to handle this task, he has also selected the best people to act as spies in the PSR. Do you know what makes for a good informant? I can tell you, bravery and the willingness to stick out one's neck too far is not on the list of qualifications. As for your other point, you're right. It will take us a long time to get out West. The logistics alone are a nightmare. Ten years and we're only now going across the river. Therefore, our plan involves flying you over enemy territory and parachuting in."

"Hell, no. No way. Their drones are our drones and our drones are good. Any plane we send over there will get shot down and anything that comes out of it will get blown up with it. We'd have to go on foot."

"So you'll do it?"

"I didn't say that. As far as I'm concerned, despite how smart you seem to think you are and how much faith you put into this talking appliance, you don't know anything about what it's like out there. Three thousand miles at least between here and there and I doubt it's any better out there."

Mercer's good humor melted away and his face hardened. It seemed that he wasn't used to being told no.

"I apologize if you were under the impression that you had a choice. You are going there, you are killing Sidney Posner, and after that, you can do whatever else you want with the years you have left in this world. I hope you can appreciate the situation I have you in. Right now, Mr. Donahue is on his way to your home to escort your mother to a new, luxury apartment close to this very spot. So close in fact, that from a lower floor, I could peer into the bedroom. As far as he knows, he is doing this to help you prepare for your journey. You are certainly correct that there is a great utility, having a mad dog at your leash. Faster than it would take for you to kill me, which I know would be very quick, THEO can send instruction to Mr. Donahue to unleash the beast as it were. So, I suggest you go to your new home, say your goodbyes, and hit the road."

Michael had underestimated the business magnate. All he could do was snarl and bite his tongue. He may have been waiting for her to die, but not like that. No one deserved that. And while he was gone, Michael knew he could figure some kind of revenge. Some retribution for the man who had him bent over a barrel. And the talking toaster, too.

CHAPTER SIX

Michael left the Olympus, grabbing the address to his new home on his way out. He hurried down the block to find a pre-fall building that oozed luxury and the comforts of the modern world. A collection of glass and steel, out front, its green canopy read "The Lovecraft" in gold letters. He was almost impressed, but it was nothing more than a fancy jail cell. He breezed past the security guard on duty, up yet another elevator to the eighth floor and as the doors closed, Michael heard an instrumental humming. Music. The elevator had music. It was as if he'd awoken in the year two-thousand and eighteen.

He marched down the carpeted hall to apartment number eight-o-five, whose door was adorned with gold, cursive lettering, and a peephole. To the side of the door was an ivory-colored doorbell surrounded by an ornate, gold frame that looked freshly polished. Michael thought about pressing but decided to barge in and stop whatever the hell was going on inside. Twisting the knob, he burst through shoulder first, as if expecting some great stone lying behind it that he would have to account for. Instead, the light wooden door almost fell out of its screws and looked like a broken cabinet, hanging on by a few screw threads.

"How is that any way to enter a room? I swear, you should have stayed in that shit hole since it's apparent you don't know how to behave in civilization. Animal! Neanderthal!" she raved. "At least I'll have some peace and quiet while you're away."

She knew. That was going to make things hard, Michael figured. She was a stubborn pain in the ass who wanted to live in an apartment like this since Michael had forced her out of their house. It was a nice place, too. That would make it harder still. At least fifteen hundred square feet. Three bedrooms. Two baths and a large kitchen. A terrace with a balcony that she could use to feed her nicotine addiction without infecting the rest of the place. A few empty picture frames waiting to be filled.

"Your mom is a piece of work, Mike. Not at all what I expected," Donahue announced, coming out of one of the bedrooms. "When I came by with a couple of Mercer's goons, she had a nine mil pointed right at my balls. Almost shat my pants," he laughed.

"She's always had good instincts. Probably why she's still alive," Michael replied.

"No thanks to you," she sniped, putting away the few plates she had into a cupboard above the sink.

Donahue wore a knowing smile, like he'd just finished picturing some cruel, violent demise for the Conner's family. Michael noticed the faintest droplets of blood running off his chapped lips as if he'd been lightly nibbling them.

"Didn't I tell you we were going to make a big payday, Mike? Didn't I say it when I left Mercer's office?"

"You weren't in there long. What did you talk about?"

"Not much", Donahue replied with nonchalance. "He told me that this Posner guy has to go, I gave him a price, we shook, and then he asked me to escort your mom over here."

"Did he give you anything?"

"Half my fee in D-Coin on the spot. More than I'd make in ten years. Makes me almost want to say fuck it and runoff, you know? But I figure he must be good for the rest."

"Hey," Michael said to his mother, "you mind giving us the room? I want to talk about some things you probably shouldn't be hearing."

"My own home and I can't be in the room. You've got some nerve. I gotta use the bathroom, anyway, so go ahead, talk about who shot JFK and where they buried Hoffa for all I care," she said as she shuffled to the bathroom on the other side of the apartment.

Michael grabbed Donahue by the collar and slammed him against the wall. "What did he tell you about her? Did he tell you to hurt her? To hurt me?"

Donahue had a bewildered expression. "Hurt you? I'd never do that, Mike. Why would I hurt you? You're my best friend."

Michael let go and Donahue straightened himself out. The shocked look on his face went morose. "You're the only guy on the team who doesn't judge me. I tell a story or do something they think is fucked up and they all look at me like an animal. But you always look at me the way you look at a hot piece of ass or children playing or a bloodbath. Hell, you even look at your own Mom the same way. Same expression. No judgment. You and me are the only guys who know how to survive in this country. Everyone else is trying to bring it back to how it was before. But us, we know that this is how it's always really been. And everything else was a fantasy."

Michael looked down at his hands, small beads of sweat were forming on his palms. The toilet flushed and shuffling feet were fast approaching. Donahue dusted himself off, his uniform disheveled.

"I think a lot of bad thoughts. Most of the time, I just do whatever I think will feel good. I'll admit I thought about your mom in some ways that you wouldn't like. But I wouldn't want to hurt you. You're the only friend I have. When we got picked for this job, I was happy it wasn't Caroline or Gomez or Chief. Even Newbie looks at me like he's better than me. Nah," he started wagging his index finger, "this is fate. It's all meant to be like this."

Michael's mother came out of the bathroom, cigarette lit and between her lips, shuffling back to the kitchen, continuing her move-in. Michael, somewhat perplexed, walked over to the glass door that led out to a small terrace. He stared out the window, thinking. Best friend? Fuck.

"I'm going to wait downstairs, Mike. I figure you've got it from here," Donahue added as adjusted the front door so that it could close behind him.

Michael waited a minute after the door closed, then moved through the apartment in a frenzy.

"Okay, we don't have any time for arguing. Pack a bag of the bare essentials, we need to get out of here,"

"No, I don't think we do," she replied in a calm tone as she organized the silverware drawer. Her hard look was gone and there was a warm glint in her eyes that Michael remembered when he was younger. "That man told me you're going to California for some damned reason or another."

"He thinks we are, but we can sneak out the back and get somewhere safe if we're quick. Maybe even Canada if we hit the right part of the border. If anything we can talk to Jake. You might need to pretend to like gefilte fish, but it's better than the alternative. So get your things and let's move."

"You can find Daisy while you're there."

"I can't go find Daisy because I'm not going to California, now come on. I won't ask again!" he threatened.

"No!" she shouted, slamming a plate on the marble countertop. Shards of cheap ceramic flew in the air like shrapnel from a grenade. There was a small cut on her hand that looked like it had only sliced through a few capillaries. She took a paper towel and applied pressure as she composed herself, lifting her cigarette out of the tray and taking a drag that left about a centimeter of ash in its wake.

"You are going to California. You are going to find my daughter and bring her back to me. I haven't seen her in so many years and I know that I don't have a lot of time left. I'm old, fat, and sedentary. People half my age, hell a quarter of my age are dying from all manner of horrors. I know my time is coming. But, don't worry about that. I'll live long enough to see her safe and sound."

"My sister," Michael murmured.

"What was that?"

"She's not just your daughter, she's my sister. And for reasons I can't get into right now, you are going to have to just trust me when I say that I can't go to California. I am your son and I am trying to protect you. Let me."

She tapped the ash into the tray, then rubbed the butt into it, smothering away its last embers. "My son is dead. You. You're something else entirely."

"You're impossible," Michael said in frustration.

"You know what's impossible? Raising a good, perfect little boy who laughed and smiled all the time. Then watching him grow up into a man and seeing him go off to war. I read the news. Every Day. I see the names in the paper every day. I hope and pray I don't see his and every day, I breathe a sigh of relief and then worry about tomorrow's paper. And then I got my boy back. Despite the odds. Despite all the other mothers who lost their sons. All the news stories of other people's sons and daughters getting killed, I thought God blessed me with a miracle. But you walked through the door, looking around like some kind of predator. Looking at me like you were thinking of ways to hurt me. And I knew my son was gone. And some kind of machine took his place. A monster wearing my beautiful boy's face. I used to love his green eyes. Now, I look into yours and see nothing. No spark. No joy. Every day, I stare at a walking, talking corpse, desecrating my boy's face. I haven't seen his smile in years. I can't even look at photographs without seeing you instead. My son had a sister. You, whatever you are, have a job now. I'm begging you. If any piece of my son still lives inside that husk. If I'm wrong and there is some kind of spark, please, bring my daughter back to me."

Michael said nothing, staring blankly at her face. He was waiting for some insult. Some kind of tell that she wasn't serious. But it never came. Tears formed in the corners of her eyes and traveled down her wrinkled cheeks, meeting at her bony chin and falling to the floor, like bursting bombs exploding onto the wooden floor below.

"This place isn't all it's cracked up to be," he replied after a protracted silence.

"There are worse places," she countered. "I'm sure you'll see many of them."

"They'll basically have you as a prisoner, you know. And if I don't come back, they might even kill you."

"I'm not worried about that. I've hoped and prayed for a long time that you'd die out there and that my son would know peace, but you always came back. God has some kind of plan for you and no one goes before it's their time."

"I mess this up, you're dead."

"There are worse prisons."

"I don't even know if-," he started.

"She's alive. I know it. It's my job to know."

"When dad, I mean, when your husband died, I wish that I'd-I mean, I'm sorry that I wasn't-"

"Stop. My husband was lucky. If he would have seen you, as you are now, he'd probably kill himself all over again. He loved Michael. I'm sure you know that. Deep down, you know that Michael was loved."

Michael did know. The logical parts of his brain described the feelings he was missing out on, in much the same way that the blind remember what colors looked if they could see at some point. Trips to the beach. Birthday parties. Snow days. Michael Connors had lived a full and wonderful childhood. But proper sacrifices aren't the things people can do without.

"I had a reason for what I did. With my head and the war and all that."

"I don't want to know. As far as I'm concerned, the US government took my son and lobotomized him to fight their wars. I refuse to believe he'd give them that willingly."

But I did, Michael thought. We all did. And with better luck and circumstance, you might have never known any of it.

"If I do find her-"

"When", she interrupted.

"If I do find her, I'll ask her to come back with me. I'll leave it up to her. It may be that she can't just pick up and go. For all I know, she has her own family by now. She'd be old enough."

"If that's true, then a letter would suffice. Something of hers I can hold and be buried with and that will let me know she's okay. And here, give her this," she said, taking the gold crucifix from around her neck and placing it in Michael's hand.

"Her father gave it to me when we started dating. I had so much more in the old house, but you told me to leave it all. My mother had the most beautiful diamond earrings and my husband had this ugly watch he insisted on always wearing."

"I remember that watch. It had roman numerals around the face and a blue, Velcro strap. I always assumed he'd bought it at a pharmacy or something like that."

"His brother gave him that watch when they were kids. He was so sentimental. Tried to keep everything. Every little note I wrote him, he kept. Every report card. Every hand made father's day present. When he died, I looked through the drawer in his nightstand, full of those notes I wrote him. I had to leave them in the house, too."

Michael didn't know about the notes. He wondered if he'd kept all the letters he'd written in boot camp. Or the postcard he wrote from his summer at Lake Champlain. He remembered all of these things as they were, with no tinge of emotion to cloud the events. If he were to write it all down, it would read like the technical manual to a happy childhood.

"She's in Silicon Valley. Or at least, that's where she last was. I remember an email she sent me before all this happened. It had an address. She asked me to send her some clothes she didn't pack. I was going to get around to it that week, but then it all went away."

"I'll do my best. That's the capital of the PSR. Probably the most dangerous place for me to be."

"I don't care. And I know that you don't either. I've seen you sitting in that cot at night, waiting. It's no way for someone to live, just waiting for it to be over. Do this for me, please. Or-"

"Or?"

"Or don't come back here. Don't make me have to see my son's face again without any life in it. Please."

He approached the old woman, with tears in her eyes and he spread his arms wide, then closed around her shoulders. She felt so frail in his arms, not like how he'd remembered her those years before. The lack of a balanced diet, her cancer, and the stress of life post-May Day could wither the strongest soul. But, to his surprise, she mustered the strength to wrap her arms around him, too. It was the first hug she'd given him in years and although it did nothing for him, in those moments he tried to suppress those dark thoughts that wondered how much pressure it would take to snap her in half.

"I'll do it," he said between his teeth. Then he turned around and made for the door.

"Wait, won't you need anything? That man packed a bag for you."

"I've got some things downstairs. Thanks," as he left the apartment. She followed and watched him march to the elevator.

"Thank you, Michael," she whispered. He pretended not to hear her and as the elevator doors closed, he saw the same look she'd given him all those years ago when he was still himself.

CHAPTER SEVEN

Most stretches of I-80 were the same. A rapidly declining two-lane interstate flanked by trees, a natural tunnel overtaking mankind's attempt to conquer nature. The highway median was overgrown and sprouted mobs of wildflowers of muted purples and blood reds. The occasional zephyr swept their spores in the air, invading the woods that crept towards the cracking blacktop road. The asphalt had taken years of rain, snow, sleet, and ice with no one to maintain it and though it could still service vehicles, it'd be a bumpy, uncomfortable ride. They found the highway mostly empty save for a few cars and the occasional Semi-Truck. One was a Deluge Driver-less model. When Michael and Donahue peered inside the trailer, they'd found it already plundered.

"Where the fuck are we?" Donahue asked.

"Pennsylvania," Michael answered.

"Still?"

They'd been walking for a week and on occasion, saw a highway sign with offramps to small cities or Podunk towns that were probably hostile to outsiders. Several signs called the interstate the Z.H. Confair Memorial Highway. Michael had no idea who Z.H. Confair was and would probably forget the Highway's namesake until the next time he saw it. He wondered if anyone would ever know who Z.H. Confair was again. They stopped one evening off the banks of a river, under the highway bridge that spanned it. Michael washed himself but was unable to catch anything out of the river save for an old Pennsylvania license plate that read "FISHIN" of all things. He left it on the banks of the river, where it would most likely stay until the water swelled and brought it back where it had come from.

"We should have used a car," Donahue moaned. "We could have done P.A. in a day tops."

"If we had a day's worth of gas, then sure. But that attracts all kinds of unnecessary attention."

"Like some assholes carrying a pink AR-15 isn't already screaming 'hey look at me'."

He had a point, Michael thought as he cradled the rifle he'd found a few days back, an ugly abortion of a thing that was no doubt expensive, but lacking in both aesthetics and practicality. There'd been a trend in gun collecting circles, people painting their rifles in all kinds of loud colors. Gaudy golds, baby blues, fire engine reds, everything except basic black it seemed. This particular firearm was bubblegum pink and had the extra annoyance of being made with skeletonized parts, which meant that if nothing else, Michael would always have something to do since dust invaded every nook and cranny. At one point, it had a unicorn key chain hanging off the charging handle, but Michael dispatched with that monstrosity as soon as he'd seen it. Michael hated the thing, but it fired true and he had enough rounds to keep her dangerous until he found something better.

"So how are we gonna do it?" Donahue asked. He'd been asking with great frequency since they left, how they'd kill Sidney Posner, and each time, Michael responded with an "I don't know" and a shrug. Though he had a long patience, the constant asking was getting on his nerves and if he had any sense of humor, he'd say that if Donahue didn't stop, he'd turn them around and go home. Instead, the shrug, but Michael knew that deep inside, somewhere, he was hilarious, even if he hated jokes.

Another day passed and Donahue was certain that they hadn't made any progress at all until they hit the first highway sign that read "State Border". Crossing into Ohio, a rusted road sign high above the interstate read "Ohio: Find it here". If only, Michael thought, as the pair crossed into the Buckeye State. It was another day by the time they hit Cleveland and Donahue had been dancing a jig when they reached the city limits.

They found lodging for the night in an old house-turned museum. It had served as the set for an Old Christmas movie that Michael remembered watching as a kid. Every year, one of the channels would play the movie on repeat for twenty-four hours. His family would play it in the background of the day's festivities and it would not be unusual to see the movie in its entirety throughout the day at least once, if not more so. The house was yellow inside and out and the main living room had been converted into some kind of gift shop. An old novelty lamp designed to look like a woman's leg in fishnet stockings stood tall in the window, to which Donahue remarked, "I'd love to meet the rest of her." They climbed the stairs to find a loft apartment on the third floor that looked like a modern home, with all the conveniences of the world before May Day.

"Spooky, eh?" Donahue asked.

"Not really. We've been in empty houses before."

"No, I mean the Museum. This apartment looks like any other place in the world, but that place downstairs was supposed to look like the nineteen-thirties. It'd be easier living in that kind of place than it would be living in this apartment."

"Let's get some sleep before you philosophize your way to an aneurysm."

Donahue mean mugged as he pulled out the sleeper sofa in the living room. Michael took the master bedroom. The bed was bare, but he'd found extra sheets in the closet as well as the pillows and blankets. He hadn't tried sleeping in over a week, much longer than he'd ever tried previously, and felt like he could keep going, but decided not to find out how long he could go. His weary body welcomed the rest and he slept for six hours, a personal best. Morning beat Michael for the first time in years and the sun peeking onto his face found him fresh for the day's walk. Michael sauntered out of the bedroom as Donahue lay sleeping on the sofa.

"You'd better get up," Michael chastised.

"I've been up for an hour. Tried going back to sleep, but this mattress pad sucks."

"You've slept in worse."

"Slept with worse, too. Cleveland today?"

"Yup."

"Caravan today?"

"Probably."

"We ought to come up with a back story. Two military-age males walking into town together while every Recruiter should be chomping at the bit for us doesn't bode well, I figure."

He was right. Michael hated to admit it, but he needed that psycho to get through this. Maybe even more than that Psycho needed him. When Donahue called him his best friend, Michael cringed. Were they really that similar? He wondered.

"I'll be a salesman. My father was a salesman."

I can't be a truck driver, Michael thought. Those cross-country trips were getting longer and longer as Michael grew older. The automated trucks were taking all the local work. They were cheaper, faster, and by some accounts, safer. Cross country work was still a human endeavor, though. But that didn't last long. When they found him, he was in the garage. He'd always joked that the air didn't seem right if it didn't taste like exhaust. The car was still running and he got himself comfortable, his seat leaned all the way back and his feet away from the pedals. It was clear that he'd been crying.

"I guess I'll be a Plumber."

They made it to the city center, passed the ballpark where the Indians used to play. Michael's friend Brandon was drafted by the Indians out of College. He only played in one major league game, which was more than most people could say. Brandon was out of his mind just as fast as he'd come in as they arrived at a small park with a few monuments to the City's history. A sitting man labeled Tom Johnson looked over a boomerang-shaped plot of dead grass with the occasional dandelion, mirrored by a war memorial. A man wearing a sash that said "information" flagged the pair down with friendly excitement. He wore thick glasses, a bushy gray mustache, and genial smile.

"Welcome, gents. Name's Eli Boone. I am the head of the Cleveland City Welcoming Committee, Chairman of the Citizens Alliance, and interim Mayor while we sort things out here," he hollered at them with the same exuberance that puppies greet their masters with.

"Howdy," Donahue belted back at him, feeding off the old man's energy. He was a pencil-thin man with more hair than face and a pair of glasses so thin that Michael thought they were for show. The eccentric civic leader looked like a caricature, which heightened Michael's already astronomic suspicions about most everyone he met. That he was sans pants made the ensemble all the more.

"All new citizens of Cleveland are allotted a home, some rations, and a job around town. We just need to get you sorted down by my office. Follow me to City Hall," he announced as he started marching away, presuming the pair would follow. He didn't look back once as he rambled on about the city and its history, while Michael and Donahue stayed put, looking at one another with dumbfounded amazement.

"You don't see that shit every day," Donahue figured.

The pair meandered around the city streets, looking for other signs of life besides their bare-legged Mayor, stopping outside an old-fashioned Saloon with a California Flag hanging off the pole over the front windows. As they entered, it carried the same shit hole vibe as the Gracie Pub. The front window was stained glass that had built up a large level of grime and dust, making it less than fit for purpose. Most of the high-top tables had no chairs and a few of the stools looked more tilted than a rigged pinball machine. The only source of light in the whole establishment was a string of construction lamps that was powered by an old gas generator. Most of the town seemed to run on these types of generators as throughout, they created a dull hum around town that Michael first thought was some kind of dying, sick animal wailing from not so far away. The bartender, whose second eye worked as well as the first, poured them both a shot of Crown Royal.

"I prefer tequila," Donahue complained.

"We've got this or Labatt Blue beer."

"Fucking Canadians," Donahue grumbled, taking the shot and hoisting it back. No kind of exchange was mentioned or expected as the bartender gave a simple nod, communicating in one gesture, more kindness than Michael or Donahue were capable of expressing in words. Michael held onto the glass and sipped the shot glass, savoring the sensation that burned in the back of his throat.

"Don't knock'em. Canadians are keeping this place afloat 'til things get better."

"By the looks of your Mayor, seems like you've got quite some time until then."

"Ah, don't mind Eli. He's a sweet old man. Couldn't harm anyone. He used to come round all the time but when the lights went out, he got it in his mind that he could bring things back in order. Poor guy, he was never really all there to start. Wish I could say he was the only one. Or the worst for that matter. That's an interesting rifle you've got there, friend. Mighty bold to be sporting colors like that."

"I saw that flag out front", Michael replied, "Mighty bold to be flying those colors anywhere east of the Rocky Mountains."

"Fair enough," he laughed, setting up the next round.

"Caravans run out of here then?" Donahue asked.

"Yeah. They come through every few weeks or so. One's set to leave in a couple of days as a matter of fact. The guy should be by sooner or later. Told me to keep the drinks free and mention it to whoever comes in. Like I'm their spokesman or recruiter or something."

A lucky break, Michael thought. They drank and just as the glasses hit the pine, the bartender set them up another round and they toasted their host. A few more rounds passed as they toasted everyone from Eli Boone to Tom Johnson to Lebron James. A few hours passed when the door opened and a short, fit man with squared sunglasses walked in and took a seat at a large table in the back.

"That's Joe. He's a Coyote for the PSR. He's a real gung-ho party guy if you get me. Just don't get him started on politics. My ears just stopped bleeding."

Michael nodded his head and the pair walked over to Joe's table and asked to sit.

"No need to ask, Citizen. It's a free country. Well, it will be anyway."

They sat and the bartender came by with another round, as well as a bucket of beers.

"Citizen Dylan Dougherty. You couldn't be more Irish if you had a potato growing out of your forehead and shat shamrocks as you walked. How've you been?"

"Fine, Joe, fine. I was just telling these guys that you're the guy who takes people where they want to go."

"The promised land, Citizen Dylan. The promised land. You know," he said, raising his eyebrow, "they say that where California goes, America follows. It's inevitable. We took our independence and now we're looking to free our fellow Americans. Then, when we've got everything where it needs to be, we can start the long march East."

"Probably have to change the name. Pacific States doesn't have much play on the Atlantic", Michael rebutted.

"Nonsense, Citizen…?"

"Connors. Michael Connors."

"Nonsense Citizen Michael Connors. Pacific means more than our West coast ocean. We mean to bring peace back to the continental United States. To Pacify it, if you will. And to do that, we've got to shave some of the older, less enlightened aspects of our history. A new birth of freedom requires a new foundation. New foundation requires a new name, no?"

Michael didn't care one way or the other but held his discontent close to the chest. It was easy. He'd just sit and be quiet and nod when appropriate. He felt like he was back in the army, where dozens of other motivated soldiers echoed the same enthusiasms that Joe professed right now. Michael had such enthusiasm once, but he found that it retreats as experience pushes its way in.

"How many trips have you made cross country?" Donahue asked. He was all business, which Michael found refreshing.

"I don't usually answer questions posed by strangers."

"Donahue," he dropped like it was infected with something.

"Three Irish in one place. Maybe I shouldn't take you at all, or you leave a trail of shamrocks behind," he laughed, but no one joined him. " As to your question, Citizen Donahue. Once here and two out to Pittsburgh."

"We passed Pittsburgh. Deluge Army was occupying it," Michael added. They hadn't passed through there, but the intel reports they read before the trip said as much.

"Which is why I've come to Cleveland. This'll probably be my last time here. Retreat across Route Eighty, giving them a scent of us, til we've got those corporate, fascist drones right where we want them. Imagine it. They march their slave army to every city across the Midwest, find them empty, and as they reach the Rockies, they get overrun by the people they wish to subjugate. It's almost poetic. They don't have enough Reps to handle that reckoning, I can tell you that."

He spoke with the venom of a viper's den, his hatred not quite fanatic, but teetering towards that edge. It would be smart to avoid this man, Michael thought. But he knew the best way West, where to avoid and what lay beyond their immediate horizons. Michael's road map might as well read "there be monsters" in all the places he had yet to venture.

"When do we leave?"

"Caravan's camped outside of the city. We'll leave in a few days."

"Pittsburgh is only a two-day walk from here. Shouldn't we get a move on?" Donahue asked.

"You boys don't know much about these slavers do you?"

"Just that I'd rather not meet them," Michael answered.

"Indeed," Joe laughed. "Well, they aren't going to come here for quite some time, I can tell you that. Pennsylvania is a huge forest littered with mountains. They take Pittsburgh and then need to cover their flanks in case your local partisans or average folk who don't want to be caught in all this mess try to monkey wrench their plans. Plus, they'll go to all the local towns and look under every rock to find more able bodies for their armies. So yeah, they could spear drive their tanks and trucks and humvees all the way to Colorado in twenty-four hours, but they don't know what we've got waiting for them along the way. The day they try to take Cleveland in fact, they'll find all sorts of fun surprises waiting for them."

Joe gave them directions to the camp on the other side of the Cuyahoga River, writing out a note for them to give to the quartermaster. When they arrived, they found no such person existed, as the campsite looked more like a Hooverville than a military camp. There were a few makeshift brick and sheet metal structures and tens of poorly built tents scattered all about. The people, Michael's fellow travelers, did not look like they could make such a journey, especially at the pace Michael felt comfortable with. He was sure that most would die off along the way. Starvation, exhaustion, exposure, disease. And that was just Mother Nature's arsenal.

"I'm gonna check out the local talent," Donahue proclaimed, marching off, schmoozing with those Michael had just signed off as the walking dead.

A few children were running around, chasing a small, malnourished boy with fair blonde hair and wearing a beat-up pair of overalls. His old sneakers had a cartoon character on them that Michael didn't recognize. The Velcro straps that secured the shoe to the boy's feet were full of mud and sand and only a few tiny threads were holding the strap in place over the tongue. As he stepped, a faint red light shone from the heel.

The children caught the small runner and surrounded him, closing in like a pack of wolves around a wounded deer. Michael didn't remember that part of Bambi, but took a few steps over and shot a glare at the obvious ring leader, who was a good foot taller than the others. The boy tried to avert his gaze and pretend that Michael wasn't there, but like the old wives' tale about snakes, he could mesmerize those who met him until their blood stopped flowing, frozen in the veins. The tall boy backed up and turned tail, followed by his cronies. The small boy, much to his surprise, looked around to see if he was indeed responsible for the feat. Michael was halfway across the camp when he heard the distinct wheezing laugh of old, sick men. He turned to see to geezer, hunched over on a crate-turned-stool. He was playing checkers with another old man, who was quieter and averted his gaze from any and all who looked on him. A small, white, and gray cat lay next to his feet, unperturbed by the putrid stench the two old men produced.

"Something funny?"

"Yep," he replied, baring a once toothy smile.

"You wanna share?"

"That boy ought to keep you around. Might even keep the crows off his crops, man."

Michael was a few feet from the old-timer, yet his presence could waft to the other end of the camp and possibly the outer edge of Cleveland.

"I don't like unfair fights. Except when I fight unfair."

That made the old man laugh even harder. His long white beard had a thick braid that almost touched the ground as he sat. He was thin, but wiry and probably quite a bit stronger than most men his age and probably half the men half his age. There was a faded, green tattoo on his exposed upper arm that looked like some sort of skull wearing some kind of hat, though Michael could barely tell because of his sun-baked, wrinkled skin. The man gave off what some called an "aura" and Michael felt less on edge around him than he did most people, which surprised him. He was one that would make it.

"Hey, if fightings your thing, that's your thing, I guess. I figured with a groovy-looking gun like that, you were more of the peace-loving type. But, I've been wrong before. Just know I'm not your enemy, Brother. I just think there are more people out there than preteens, is all, man. Though you're a rough looking guy. Maybe you've made your way through all the fighters and need to pick on some preteens," he laughed.

"I don't see many pacifists with skull tattoos." The old man went almost epileptic with laughter after that one and actual tears started streaming down his face.

"Jerry Garcia would be rolling in his grave, hearing you say that, man. Funny though. Not many people can tell what she is anymore, even though the roses should give it away."

"Stumped me."

"You come on over to my tent and I'll introduce you to the Grateful Dead. By the look of you, seems like you could stand to chill out. Too much on the brain. Too much tension in that brow, Man."

"Some other lifetime, maybe," Michael replied, as he walked from the old man, who howled on at the response. The next couple of days passed without event. He saw the old man a few times when the communal meals were served, though Michael only acknowledged him with a few choice nods. The gang of children and the small boy in the overalls kept distance between themselves and Michael hadn't slept since that last time in the museum. Normal had been established.

CHAPTER EIGHT

Michael waited in line for his first of three dollops of gray goop, whose makeup and nutritional information did not exist on the side of its industrial-sized packaging, nor had it any identifying marks. The sour, surly woman serving it, whose mechanical movements included "scoop, turn, and shake", was probably no wiser to the meal's true name. The common parlance was "slop" and that seemed to suit the "food" fine. It was they who had to consume it and all the slop had to do was wait until its tortured existence was extinguished by the starving camp denizens. It tastes like mashed, wet cardboard, drowned in salt and its soupy consistency would sit in the lower intestine until just after the lunch portion was consumed, then asking to be dropped from the bowels like a cement block at the earliest convenience.

He sat far from the rest, observing rather than engaging in the mindless chatter and ignorant optimism that teemed throughout. Michael, hardened, cynical, and robotic, did not want to draw suspicion on himself by raining on their collective parade. It was dangerous to be outnumbered. Even more dangerous to be outnumbered by the desperate.

After breakfast, Michael went down to the river, a custom he'd grown used to in only a few days. He saw the Austrian student, Werner speaking to one of the horses. Michael spoke no German but could recognize the 'Lego language' and its particular sound and syntax. Most found German to be a coarse, harsh, and ignoble language, but Michael found kinship with the words that Werner was saying. He was soft, yet firm with the beast, petting its mane while having a tight grip on the reigns.

"Herr Michael, good morning," Werner called out, walking over to him. Michael had been caught staring, now drawn into an unwanted encounter.

"Morning," he replied, hoping to evade him like the Stasi.

"Ohio is quite beautiful, isn't it? This river reminds me almost of the Danube."

"This river used to catch on fire."

"Oh? How fascinating! And now it is safe to drink from?"

"Safer than dehydration."

Werner started saying something to the horse.

"Why do you speak German to the horses?"

"Not all of them. Just Johann. The other horses don't understand German. Johann didn't come from California. He was brought here by the Amish couple. They let me take Johann to the river." He paused for a moment. "I was a student here before. I've been stuck here for five years, with no one else to talk to in my natural language. I thought that they would know some German, but they can only read it in their bible. Johann is the only creature I've met that does not look at me like I have two heads and five ears."

"Five years is a long time away from home."

Werner spoke at a slow pace, choosing every word with precision. His accent was faint and fading. Michael wondered if he thought in German anymore or if that, too, was fading from his mind. How difficult it would be for him to come home after waiting so long, just to not fit in. To let the seeds of anticipation grow further and further from reality, only to find that when it came time to harvest, a barren patch of dirt remained. There was much hope in Werner's eye and though he seldom felt, Michael was not cruel. He would not take the young Student's hope from him.

There was a commotion at the campsite and the two walked back to find Joe on top of a wooden wagon, gathering everyone around in a school circle. The old man took a seat next to the other gray-haired hippie. The gang of boys and the little runt sat around the surly woman who served all the meals. Michael noticed the Amish couple that Werner had mentioned, the man staring bullets through Michael's skull. The rest of the crowd were just faces, people Michael either had not met yet or had no plans to meet. All of them, waiting to hear what the coyote had to say.

Joe was flanked by a couple of other PSR organizers, a woman named Anne and a man, Jose. Michael had learned fast that everything said in camp got back to Joe via Anne. She walked like a ghost, haunting any small group that formed, picking up even the slightest gossip that could be gained. Gathering intelligence was difficult to work and Michael lauded her for her mastery but knew to keep his distance. Jose, meanwhile, seldom spoke and instead was keen on keeping watch. He carried an old hunting rifle with him, with iron sights and a worn-out parade sling. The triumvirate towered over their flock imposing stability and authority that most had not known for some time.

"We're setting off today," he began. He let the mood shift under the weight of his words before he continued. "You are to pack lightly and are only permitted to take the essentials. I can assure you that no material item will make the difference between living and dying. Only we can do that. If you listen to us and do as you're told, you will make it to the promised land and gain the freedom of citizenship in the Pacific States Republic. If not, I will personally dispatch you. At least one of you will try to steal from the rest of us. At least one of you will try to rape, murder, or otherwise harm another member of the caravan. It happens every time. This is your warning. Don't be the one. You will die. And you will live up to your life's ultimate purpose, buzzard food, and varmint shit."

Michael scanned the faces of the others, looking for the probable offenders. Donahue came to mind, but he was on the clock, and though ruthless, he wasn't stupid. He locked eyes with the Amish man, who was still staring him down. He'd never met the man before but was being glared at with the indignant familiarity that victims hold toward their perpetrators. Maybe it would be Werner. He looked harmless, though Michael held suspicions towards harmless men. It was always the harmless men that made the biggest messes, he found. The old man wasn't harmless. He could handle himself, but he kept his sword sheathed. On display for all to see, but never drawn unless provoked. If he could like people, the old man would be someone Michael liked.

He went face by face, judging everyone in the crowd, finding little flaws in their character, real or imagined. One lady smiled too much, while one man did not smile at all. Michael assumed that one man's short stature would make him envious of all those who towered over him. Michael worried that the fat woman down the row would hoard and steal food, though it was very likely that she wouldn't make it and if she did, there was even less reason to believe that she'd still be fat by the end.

"But what about me?", Michael went inward as Joe droned on. He spoke quickly and for a long time, yet said very little. Through the propaganda were useful bits of information that were probably lies. Michael thought about the ease with which he found his line of work. He made deliveries, much the same as millions of others around the world. Where some wore brown shorts, Michael wore a modified policeman's uniform. Or at least he did. This was his last delivery. He'd bring death to Sidney Posner for a small fortune, then retire, knowing that if the world got any worse, it wouldn't be his fault for once.

There was a commotion around the camp as people decided what could stay and what could go. Children chose between favorite toys. Valuable heirlooms were tossed away like garbage. One man, a One woman clung to a few photo albums like they were nursing on her breast. Her husband, cooing, tried to take them from her.

"Amelia, please! They're too heavy."

"They're all we have left of him," she cried. "Of any of them. I can't. I won't leave him again!"

"Take out a few pictures and put them in your pack. Baby, please. We have to go now."

"You can take them!" she said, sniffling. "They aren't that heavy. You can put them in your backpack."

"I don't have any room for them!" he snapped. "He's gone! They're all gone!"

She started to bawl again. "Why are you doing this? Why are you treating me this way?"

He grabbed her by the arm, looked her in the eyes, and barked, "Put them down. We have to go."

The woman, barely hanging onto the stack with one arm, slipped and the albums fell to the ground around her. Following them, she collapsed, crying as the man tried to get her to stand back up. The photo albums were strewn about as she crawled on all fours trying to collect them again. Michael moved on from the couple, concerned with his own pack and well-being. There were a few such scenes. As a boy, Michael felt bad when he saw a homeless man in the city and remembered how that feeling melted away as he saw more and more of them.

The horses were gathered and Michael noticed Johann was being outfitted with an older, worn harness. The Amish man was raising hell at Joe for that and he could be heard clear across the camp.

"That's my harness for my horse, Mr. Joseph. You've no right to enlist him in any of your labors and take the labor that I work with my own two hands away from me!"

"We agreed, Abe. You'd let us use your horse to pull one of our carts with supplies and in exchange, we'd outfit you with your own plot when we got within our borders. What difference does it make if we swap out the harnesses?"

"I notice your horse gets to wear my harness? What makes him so worthy, other than he's pulling you and yours. I know what we agreed to, Mr. Joseph. Every day I wake up thinking I made a deal with the devil. Especially when I see the demons you've got us lodging with. Soulless men with soulless eyes, like animals, stalking me and mine."

"That's enough," Joe scolded. "What I do, I do out of necessity. I'm not accustomed to being questioned about it. Now, get to your horse so we can move out. If it becomes such a big deal, I'll swap out the harnesses when we make camp for the evening."

A short train of horse-drawn wagons filed out onto the blacktop cement road, setting off into unknown country and the dangers that followed. Those who couldn't hitch a ride were forced to walk. There weren't many, but it was easy to see who'd gained favor with the triumvirate and who was left to die. Some man might have looked at Anne the wrong way. Or maybe she looked at him. Regardless, Joe would have none of it. Maybe Jose saw something he didn't like. Not a crime, but a misdemeanor that warranted a fast-paced march as punishment. Michael learned the game quickly, where others would die before figuring it out. Everyone has a game. Everyone wants to make the rules of their reality. For now, Michael would play by Joe's rules.

As they left, Michael turned to see the woman with the photo albums still laying in the dirt. The man who'd tried to collect her was with the group, obscuring his face. Michael slung his gaudy rifle and the day-pack that carried all the items he deemed essential. It was a few hundred yards before the woman's crying was out of earshot. It was late in the morning, around ten, when they set off. This was another part of the game. Slop-filled stomachs marched across an empty highway as the sun grew more and more powerful. Sporadic cloud coverage brought reprieve from the growing intensity but was gone by noon, at the height of Sol's strength. Michael could feel the skin on the back of his neck burning. He'd been fair-skinned his whole life. He was otherwise covered but would look like a redneck for the rest of their journey. What was once a minor annoyance, easily relieved, was now an impediment. He couldn't turn his head as well, like a rusty door hinge begging for oil.

The fat woman started lagging behind. Her breathing was erratic and she'd probably be alright if she could stop to rest for a moment, but no such moment was coming. He wondered how she was still so fat over all this time. Michael had witnessed real starvation in his travels. Emaciated bodies laid up in corners of rooms, waiting for death or something less interesting. Grown men, all skin and bones, weighing less than Michael did as a pre-teen. He can still smell their breath. The dumpster hole of halitosis comes out like exhaust from a garbage truck. There were easy ways of handling those cases, but an ammo shortage put a moratorium on mercy killing. After that, it was standard procedure to count them as dead. There was no way of helping them. And yet, a miracle of miracles was right there behind him. Another few hours passed and Michael saw that she'd fallen back behind the horizon. No one had stopped to help her. She'd come alone and left that way. The first victim of this West Coast death march. First of many, but first all the same. Michael never learned her name.

The carts outpaced the walkers after a while, and they seemed to be walking along on faith that they'd know when to stop. The scorching sun boiled the highway below and the spotty cloud cover seemed to retreat to less forsaken pastures. Michael felt fortunate to wear hiking boots. Some were wearing beat-up sneakers that were more duct tape than anything else. Some with good shoes had no socks. One had a cheap, flatfooted pair of basketball shoes that were made of canvas and rubber. The blisters and cuts that such footwear would make were just another reality on the walk.

Michael noticed a young man wearing sandals. He had a small dog with him that he'd been carrying since they set off. He was thin, hungered, and looked like a light breeze could do him in. The dog, while thinning, was not going hungry and it was clear where the man's priorities lay. The small Yorkshire terrier was well behaved, quiet, and looked at its master with genuine affection. The added weight from carrying the dog slowed the man and he started to lag behind the rest. The look on his face said it all. He would not be meeting up with the fat lady. Those looks of affection continued as the man placed the dog on the ground and the two set off to catch the rest of the group. The Yorkie's small legs struggled to keep up and as the distance between the man and the group dwindled, a gap between him and the dog grew wider. The Yorkie called for his master, yipping, barking, and trying to sprint, only to tire out not long after. The man kept walking and as Michael turned to see him, he saw tears in the man's eyes. The dog took a seat on the hot road, tail wagging, tongue panting, waiting for his master to collect him, the affectionate look never leaving his face.

The day ended as abruptly as it began. The horse-drawn wagons made it to a rest area off the highway and although not much ground had been gained, there was a stark contrast between the semi-civilized Cleveland and the new badlands of Western Ohio. The walkers found them not long after, exhausted from the sheer mileage they'd put on their bodies. By the end, they were half what they were when they started. Off the highway, a few motels lined the streets, along with all kinds of reminders of the world that once was. Fast food joints with signs that used to light up, gas stations with cars still at the pumps, and all manner trucks and tractor-trailers. Joe gathered the tired masses around, feeding off of their desperate energy.

"Tonight, we camp here. Find a bed in one of the motels and make sure to requisition a blanket out of the supply cart. While dinner is being made, we'll need everyone to search high and low for anything useful. Food, medical equipment, cooking supplies. Anything you think might be useful comes here. There's a treasure trove here that hasn't been picked clean yet."

"We're exhausted," one man complained.

"And hungry," yelled another.

"Yeah, some of us had to walk!"

"There are plenty of cars here. Probably a lot of gas, too. Why don't we just leave the horse and buggy routine to Ahab over there and drive out west? Wouldn't take more than two days if we switched off drivers," another propositioned.

"What's your name, Citizen?" Joe asked, singling out the last man who spoke.

"Bradyn. Bradyn Thomas Lawson," the man replied.

"Citizen Lawson, do you believe I've led you astray? That I've lied to you and the other Citizens?"

"We can't keep walking. I can't at least. Twenty people got left behind and by the look of them, they aren't gonna get here. Maybe one or two. And I doubt anyone who got to ride in the wagons is going to give that up willingly. If we drive, we can get as many people across as fast as possible."

"The answer is no," Joe shot back. "Now please, I beg you, gather the supplies. Grab a blanket and a hot meal and rest. We have an early morning tomorrow. Citizen Cutler has the night watch."

There was grumbling in the crowd. Those that walked seethed with resentment towards those who rode. It was all another aspect of the game and each person played their position. They dispersed into small groups, surveying the stores and restaurants for anything useful. Michael wandered with three of the men he'd spent the day on the road with, though kept his distance. Lawson, the man who left his dog, a third that Michael had yet to meet, and Michael walked into the convenience store attached to one of the gas stations.

"It's bullshit, Rick," Lawson exclaimed. "That Commie fuckhead is trying to kill us. Fewer mouths to feed. Easier to move. And as far as his "leadership" is concerned, he probably doesn't want anyone driving cause it'll put him out of a job. They're all Luds over there, you know, right? Fuckers don't believe in technology or whatever. He's up to something. It's ninety degrees out and he's giving us thick ass blankets. He's even got the nerve to have a whole wagon of just supplies instead of letting some more people ride. I don't trust him. Any of 'em."

"Then why are you still here?" Rick asked. "I mean, why are you even going there at all if you hate them so much?"

Michael kept his ears open, making sure to fill his daypack with cans of ravioli, twinkies, and chocolate bars that had been left behind in the small service station. There was more left than he thought there'd be. Water, canned foods, and the putrid smell of spoiled frozen dinners. The hot dog roller had a few rotten sausages that were half-eaten by rats by the look of the teeth marks. There were a few bags of dry dog food, but Michael wasn't that desperate yet.

"I'm no fool. I'd rather take my chances with that faggot than the Reps. At least over there, I can be left alone," Lawson declared.

"How are you going to get one of those cars started?" the third man asked. He was the Dog Man and until he had a name, Michael would think of him as such. Probably even after.

"Most of these cars run great. They just have empty tanks. We poke a hole in the gas tanks of a few of the others and I bet you we have enough to get to San Fran by the day after tomorrow. Maybe the day after that."

"All I know is that fucker made me leave my dog. There was room, but that bastard, he- Winnie had to- had to- Oh my god!" He gasped and gasped, unable to breathe, but no tears came. He looked like he'd been crying since he put the dog down. The other two turned their attention to Michael, who'd just about finished filling his bag with a half-full can of decaf instant coffee.

"What about you, Frankenstein," Lawson asked Michael.

"I don't know what's out there. He does. I don't have to like him to follow him," Michael explained in his usual terse and candid manner. "Plus, he's got a guard out tonight. I bet you he's there as much to keep us in as he is to keep anything else out."

"Don't worry about the guard. I got something for him if he gives us trouble," he said, pulling out a nine-millimeter pistol that had been tucked in his pants, behind his shirt. "And if anything, that pretty little thing you've been slinging should cause him to keel over from laughing so hard."

They finished clearing the store and moved back to the motels. To get a blanket, one had to empty his pack in front of Jose and Brandon. Michael did as the others did, but the other three instead used the commotion to gather more supplies. Michael grabbed his blanket and found a room on the ground floor of the only motel that had a pool, though the water had been drained long before. He thought about finding Donahue but opted to instead enjoy the reprieve that circumstance had gifted him. Instead, he went to the bathroom mirror and recited the new phrases he'd come up with since he left New Jersey.

He laid in the bed, under the warm mylar blanket when he heard a tapping at the door. The curtains were shut, but he knew it was Lawson and the others. "Frank," Lawson whispered. "Hey, Frankenstein. We're moving out." He tapped again, but Michael didn't stir. Though emotion eluded him, Michael had cultivated a trustworthy gut feeling, one that had served him well since he was a boy. It often manifested as stomach ache of some sort and in that instance, Michael felt like his intestines had gone ten rounds with Mike Tyson. The tapping continued, but Michael stayed put.

"He's probably asleep," Rick said. "What do we do?"

"Any louder and we risk waking up the rest," Dogman replied.

A moment passed before Michael heard another tap.

"His loss. We gotta move," Lawson commanded.

They walked away from the door and for the next couple hours, Michael heard them fail at sneaking around, moving vehicle to vehicle, collecting whatever they'd need for their drive across America. Michael went to his window and saw the trio, along with two other walkers. They commiserated around a Ford SUV that had to be at least fifteen years old. Michael couldn't see much of their commotion but filled in the gaps by listening. He heard half-empty water jugs sloshing around with metal cans being stacked into the back of the SUV. A dull thud from a dropped gas can drew the ire of the other conspirators. Dogman was not very strong. A separate set of footsteps approached the vehicle and by either miracle or stupidity, he whispered as well.

"What the hell is going on?" Cutler asked. "Where y'all think you're going?"

"Move along. Just pretend you didn't see us," Rick implored.

"Like hell. I've got orders to keep everyone safe. Even you."

"Listen to yourself. You're not a soldier. You're not a waiter. You don't have to do what they say," Lawson reasoned. "We don't owe him or them anything."

"I don't have the luxury of thinking like that," Cutler replied. Michael could see he pulled his gun. Lawson and the others froze. "Now, we are going to all go talk to Joe. Nothing's happened except you have some food that you forgot to give to the group. No big deal. Worst that'll happen is you'll have to walk again tom-"

Gunshots broke the night's silence as Michael saw Cutler drop to the ground, blood splattered from his chest and face, oozing into a pool around his twitching body. The whispering stopped as Lawson put his pistol back and they all ran into the SUV. It took a few tries for the engine to turn over, while the others stirred from their sleep. Michael stayed inside but saw Joe and Jose run to Cutler's bleeding body. As they reached him, the SUV started and hauled ass back towards the Highway.

Jose pulled his hunting rifle, aiming at the vehicle, only for Joe to push the muzzle to the ground.

"Everyone back inside, now!" Joe yelled. "Get under a blank-" was all he could get out before a large explosion rocked the ground. Dust was kicked up everywhere and the quiet that had been previously molested crept back into the deserted truck stop. It took a few minutes before Michael could see that the SUV was engulfed in flames. Drone, Michael suspected. That explained the blankets. All that remained of the Ford was burned plastic, twisted metal, and the charred corpses of Michael's fellow travelers. Michael couldn't lay down for the remainder of the night, instead transfixed on the flames from the destroyed truck as they steadily died down throughout the night and well into the next morning.

CHAPTER NINE

Morning brought a different attitude to the caravan. Most were shaken by the night's events and it looked like hardly anyone had gotten any sleep the night before. If there were any walkers that day, they wouldn't make it. Joe walked the camp, asking everyone to gather around his wagon. He brought a sullen seriousness that Michael hadn't seen from him in the short time they'd been acquainted. As they gathered around, Michael finally was able to see how small the group had become. Where there were sixty yesterday, there were now around forty-five.

"First things first," Joe began. "We need to give our fellow Citizen, Robert D. Cutler, a proper burial. One deserving of his sacrifice to his country and all of you. Any volunteers?"

A few hands shot up. There were a couple of army spades in the supply wagon and the six volunteers almost broke into a riot fighting over who got the chance to move dirt. A few, mostly women, though a couple of men, were balling their eyes out, performing the proper mourning befitting their hero. As breakfast was being assembled, Joe spoke to the congregation of desperate migrants.

"We gather this morning to celebrate the life and commemorate the death of Robert D. Cutler, Citizen of the Pacific States Republic. I did not know Citizen Cutler well. My only interaction with him, admittedly, was when I asked if he would stand watch that night and, like all citizens of our Republic, he put the good of the many above his own comfort. In our Republic, each citizen is granted a proper funeral, much more ornate and circumstantial than this here, especially our heroes. Those who give their lives in pursuit of our ideals. Because, in the years since our founding, we have redefined what citizenship in a Republic truly means. We did not come from some far-off land, raping and pillaging and conquering. We were born on that land and realized that in order to truly be free, we must reckon with our collective past, divorce ourselves from the cancerous present and move towards a new birth of freedom. A new experiment in racial, economic, and sexual harmony awaits us past the Rocky Mountains. One where the progressive ideals that the former United States tried to enact could no longer be bastardized by the backward thinking, fear-mongering fascists that you yourselves are trying to escape. It is difficult to put into words how deep Robert Cutler's sacrifice runs. His red blood, that spilled on the ground below our feet, will one day help grow the fields green and lush and plentiful. He died as a Citizen should. A death that befits a true Citizen. Let us not make his sacrifice mean nothing. Let us continue on our path, stay the course. Let you all before me, please, listen to the wisdom I have. Look off into the distance and you can see the consequences of betrayal. The fascist drones fly above our heads and destroy anything going faster than a snail's pace. I know this. Now you know this. Citizen Cutler earned his title as a Citizen last night. May we all make the most of his sacrifice."

The congregation broke and spread like ripples in a pond, all off to gather their only possessions and meet back at the wagons, hoping that they wouldn't be one of the odd men out. A small shrine was built to commemorate Cutler, out of some small rocks and twigs. A piece of paper was rolled up in a scroll and left under a flat, round sedimentary rock. Breakfast was served, this time with the added bonus of some of the truck stop food. Michael got some ding dongs to go with his slop, which he held onto for later. He didn't care for sweets but figured that he could trade them to someone who did. He noticed the small boy he rescued before they'd all set off, staring intently at the snack cake package. Michael thought about giving it to him but worried that it was too valuable to waste on a child. The child persisted and Michael relented if only to get the boy's attention off of him. To the relief of everyone, there were enough seats in the wagons for all. They were more cramped than yesterday, which annoyed those who'd ridden, but they dare not voice any resentment. All of it, part of the game.

It took them five days to get to their next safe city, Gary, Indiana. More slop, more riding, less walking. Searching the truck stops had become routine. Michael had even systematized it. He left the obvious stuff for last. The cherry on top of his scavenger hunt. He first went behind the counter. Cigarettes were good for trading. He didn't smoke, but having lived with his mother, he knew which brands were most valuable. He'd heard about what a loosey could buy in prison and imagined that it was worth even more now. The cigarettes were first for sure. Then, he found the protein. Jerky, power bars, canned meats. These kept Michael fed. He noticed that the more he collected, the better his dinner was. No one ever came out and said that he who collects most, eats most, but Michael caught on quick and soon it became an unspoken law of the caravan.

Everything else, Michael left for other vultures. He had no need for sugar-covered chocolate donuts or cheese puffs.

Gary was an old steel town turned rust belt ghost town turned makeshift trading post. They reached the Western outskirts by the afternoon, keeping the city between them and the land they were leaving behind. Joe gathered everyone around, doing his best to keep the reigns from slipping away. The Amish man, Abe, was still raising hell about his harness and his horse and everything else. There was a general malaise all around, whether it was the bad food, how little of it was going around, not enough bathroom breaks, too many bathroom breaks. It had been a week and they made it across one state, with only wider ones ahead.

"Citizens," began Joe with his usual greeting, "We're going to lay up here for a day or two. Cleveland was just the first of a few stops on the way to our Glorious Republic." There was a collective indifference to the news. Some were happy to get the rest. Others, anxious to keep going. Michael, meanwhile, worried that he would be the odd man out again if someone needed to walk. They set up camp, this time more permanent than the hasty stations they'd been building on the road.

Michael was billeted with the Austrian kid in the handicap-accessible room next to the front office. He wasn't accustomed to company, but compared to Donahue, Werner was the perfect roommate. The room had an extra-large bathroom, which both agreed not to use unless in dire emergency. There was a cheap painting of a sailboat in between the two queen beds and a forty-two-inch television across from them on a light wood chest of drawers. Beside the window was a small desk made of the same material as the drawers with some of the motel stationary on it. Michael grabbed it and the pen that lay not six inches away and stuffed it in his pack.

Michael lay in the bed, collecting memories from all corners of his psyche. He remembered the explosion. He remembered forgetting most everything. The hospital and its paper-thin sheets, which bothered his bare ass, as they'd run out of gowns in his size. He remembered Sergeant Ross.

"Connors," Ross called out into the platoon formation. "Your bitch ass still alive?"

"Yes, Sergeant. Alive and well, hooah." Michael called back

"Custer?" he called the next name down the list. "You still dating that hooker?"

"She's an exotic dancer, Sergeant."

"Yeah, I seen that dance on Animal Planet. What the hell is wrong with you? You trying to save her for Jesus?"

"Hell no, Sarge. Jesus is gonna have to wait his turn."

Michael was back in the bed, whispering the memories, the latest of his futile ideas.

"Edwards," Michael whispered, "You still fat?"

"No, Sarge. I made weight the other day."

"You still look like a fat fuck to me."

"Hooah, Sergeant," Michael replied for Edwards.

The door opened and Werner stumbled into the room, struggling with a burlap sack of unknown contents. He dropped the bag on the floor, spilling potatoes on the dusty, dingy motel carpet.

"Herr Michael, look at what I found not so far from here. This should make breakfast more tolerable, no?"

Michael looked over at him, annoyed at the disturbance. This was the only building in their vicinity that they could adequately protect, but damn it if Michael had wished he were sleeping in a tent outside. At least there he could be alone.

"I was thinking you could bring these potatoes in for me," Werner offered. "You know, as tribute to the group. It might help with your image around here."

"Who says I need help with that?" Michael asked.

"There's been talk. Herr Joseph does not trust you. Frau Anne thinks you're suspicious. Herr Donahue says that he thinks you're..." he declined to continue.

"He thinks I'm what?"

Werner was sheepish, not wanting to look directly at Michael, who was now sitting up, drilling his gaze into the back of Werner's skull.

"He thinks..." Werner trailed off. Michael could see he was searching for the words. "He thinks you are one of 'them'." He then paused. Michael gave him a raised eyebrow. "You know, the reptiles. A spy."

That mother fucker sold me out, he thought, and though he was curious as to why the seething hatred that boiled over inside blinded him to any action other than swift vengeance. Michael got out of the bed and made for his pack, finding his knife. It had to be quiet. He left Werner without a word.

It wasn't hard finding Donahue. His pleasures included sex, alcohol, and bloodshed and while the third was unavailable, it would only increase his appetite for the others. Gary had one working bar in the whole city. Like Cleveland, it was stocked full of Canadian beer and whiskey, paid on the tab of the PSR. Michael went there and waited. It didn't take long for Donahue to walk out with a woman, his hand squeezing her arm as he dragged her along back towards the campsite. Michael hadn't seen her before. She was probably a local. Donahue knew the rules and wouldn't risk breaking them. But then, Michael thought Donahue wouldn't betray him either. They walked along the dead street, lined with cars that would never run and streetlights that would never glow with light. Michael took his time, stalking, waiting, like a deer hunter. Donahue, even when drunk and distracted, still maintained a heightened instinct for trouble, one that Michael had once relied on and now hoped had dulled. The couple stopped in front of a pharmacy and Michael could overhear them speaking.

"This is probably the only place I might find a rubber, but I'm telling you, we don't need it," he reasoned.

"No glove, no love," she slurred back at him. Donahue replied with a dismissive noise and entered the store, his paramour in tow. Michael took to an alley that lay between the building and their route, relying on sound alone to strike. They left the store a few minutes later, him laughing as they egressed.

"Welp, sorry baby, but I guess it's the old push, pull, pray tonight."

"I think I want to go home," she whined.

Listen!" he yelled. Michael heard him push her up against the store window. "Either we're fucking, or I'm fucking."

She gave no reply and they started walking again towards the alley. Michael heard Donahue's attempt to pick up the pace while she tried to slow it down. As they passed the alley, Michael saw him whip her around by the arm like an unruly dog. She attempted to swing at him, which only got him angry and he dragged her into the alley and raised a fist. Michael slipped behind and put the knife to Donahue's throat.

"Go," he told her and she ran off.

"You have no idea what the fuck you just did. Now, I'm gonna have to take out all this pent-up shit out on you."

"I very much doubt that."

"Mike?" The sound in his voice was one of deep-seated anguish that turned incredulous not a moment later. "What the fuck, man? I don't hear from you all week and now you want to fucking slit my throat because I tried to pick up a girl at a bar?"

"I don't give a fuck about her. Why'd you sell me out?"

"Woah woah woah… Settle down. Sell you out? Where'd you hear that?"

"Answer the question."

"Put down the knife and we can talk, okay? Just take it easy."

"I like it the way it is." He pressed the blade against the throat, making a light cut over where the jugular lay.

"Okay, okay, fine. Yes, I told Joe I thought you were suspicious, but he asked. While you've been doing god knows what since we got to Cleveland, I've been doing my best to earn that bastard's trust. He and the blonde think you're a spy. The Mexican says he hasn't seen you do anything suspicious. That and the fact that you've been a good little forager have kept you safe, but since that whole drone fiasco, Joe's been paranoid as fuck. He's a control freak to the nth fucking degree and the only way to keep myself in his graces was to go along with what he says."

Michael loosened the knife from Donahue's neck and pushed him away. He was ready for a fight, but nothing came of it. Donahue instead looked on Michael with deep hurt.

"Mike," he began, "I could never hurt you. I know I'm fucked up. I know that if there's something after all this shit, I'm not gonna be singing with the angels. But you're my best friend. A man has to have a line somewhere. Otherwise, he can't ever be trusted. You've trusted me with your life up til now and I thought you could do that forever. I have a plan to get you in everyone's good graces. But you gotta drop the Frankenstein act."

"Lawson called me that."

"Brother, everyone calls you that! You walk around with those dead eyes and they think you're a zombie. Anne's even said she thought you were gonna lunge at her and that almost sent Joe apoplectic."

"I've never been near her."

"That doesn't matter. There is a game going on here besides just making it. These fuckers have us all on lists and at the end of the line, it's gonna matter which one you end up on. So what you're gonna do is march over to the fire pit where Joe and some of the others hang out and dream about California, you're gonna tell them some fucking story about why you are the fuck you are and I'm gonna handle the rest, okay?"

Michael walked back to the motel and found the fire pit. Joe and Anne were there, surrounded by the Amish couple, the lady who served the food, the two old hippies, and a few others that Michael had observed with fleeting interest. He made no sound as he approached and heard the group asking Joe questions about the PSR. There were a few jumps as he made his presence known with a throat clear and all the life that had been there was sucked away, replaced by the dread that surrounds the most solemn occasions.

"I'm sorry to interrupt," Michael stated.

"Nonsense," Joe replied, getting a side-eyed glance from Anne, "All citizens are welcome, Citizen Connors."

"I know that I appear strange and distant. That I act in ways that don't mesh with what is considered normal behavior." He had their attention now, as all knew what he was talking about. "Naturally, this would raise suspicions and if there were someone else here who acted as I did, I would consider them a threat, too. But I am not a threat. I'm on a mission."

My mother just recently died and asked me to go to San Francisco and find my sister. She was at Berkeley when the world fell apart and we had no way of finding her. It's possible that she's dead, but my mother wouldn't hear it. So, I'm going out West to see. I don't feel much. Not like most other people. This whole ordeal has made me hard. Cold. I didn't come here to make friends or start a new life. I'm here to find the last reason I have to keep going through all this."

There was only silence. No one even looked like they would give a response. The crackling of the fire filled the void, and along with the sounds of bugs moving through the air. Michael left the stunned listeners behind as he went to his shared room next to the main office and found Werner sitting on his bed, deep in thought. A single tea light candle was flickering in the room on the shared nightstand between the beds.

"Herr Michael, you're back!" he exclaimed. "I thought you were gone to" but he trailed off and didn't finish the thought. He watched as Michael put the knife back in his day pack, threw off his boots, and laid down in his bed.

"Did you?… I mean, Herr Donahue is?"

"He's alive."

"Thank god. I thought that you were going to… do something unpleasant. I thought for sure you were not going to return and that Herr Donahue's life would sit on my conscience."

"If 'Herr Donahue' ever is killed, I can assure you, it won't be because of you, Werner."

They sat in the darkroom with the small flame showing only parts of their faces to one another. There was a long silence.

"You know why I call every man 'Herr' and every woman 'Frau'?

"I thought it was German for mister and miss?"

"Yes, but in Deutsch, I would call you Herr Connors, not Herr Michael. I do the first name thing because I want everyone to know that I am not an American. International students at my school were being ferried across the border to Canada after Mayday. I remember when my roommate told me. He said that he'd be going and getting out of there as quickly as he could. The day came and he had only a backpack with clothes and a couple of books. He had the most impressive collection of leatherbound books I'd ever seen. His father was an Austrian diplomat. My father stole cars and sold meth in West Virginia. I still remember the smell of those leather-bound books, with the gold-trimmed pages and the soft, yet sturdy bookmarks made of thick ribbon. He gave me a hug goodbye as he left the dorms

137

and I held him for a minute like I was never going to see him again. Long enough to show him how much he was like my own brother and long enough to swipe his wallet."

The candle flickered on and Michael could see a tear form in the corner of Werner's eye. The small pool of wax that gathered was rising around the wick and would soon drown out the flame.

"I knew what I was doing. I heard the stories. Border guards shooting people without papers or rounding them up to sell to recruiters. I remember when Canada was the benchmark for world tolerance, at least they said they were. That shit went out the window when their closest neighbor became a third-world country. Werner probably died wondering where he left his wallet. If he's alive, he's probably still trying to figure it out. Did he leave it in the dorm? Did it fall out of that jacket pocket? The picture is black and white and most people don't look at that tiny picture long enough to see that we aren't so different. I remember going to bars with my Chinese friend's ID. Swear to god."

He chuckled, then choked a bit. The wick was hovering above the wax. Darkness would consume the room in mere seconds.

"Why are you telling me this?" Michael asked.

"Because I know what you are. I saw it in your eyes tonight. I was so worried that I got another person killed and I had to tell someone. This way, you know my secret and I know yours. It's nice, to tell the truth for once. Like taking a deep breath after coming up from the bottom of a pool. But now we need to dive back down, Michael. Me the Austrian student and you the stoic traveler. I don't need to know anything else about you. Just please don't kill me. Too much has happened for me to die like this."

The candle went out and there was no more talking. Michael didn't even try to sleep that night. He only thought about what Donahue told him and what Werner had revealed. Looking back, he should have known that Werner's story was bullshit. It was obvious now that it was out in the open. He wondered if he could trust Werner. Wondered if he should even keep calling him that. Killing him would solve a few problems, but bring up a few more. At this point, it didn't matter if he were Jeffery Dahmer, Joe would ferry him across to the PSR. He could drop the charade if he wanted unless of course, his goal was to get off the continent entirely. They both revealed themselves that night, one by accident and the other out of guilt. If they were to survive, it seemed they would need to go back to the bottom of the pool and grow gills.

The next morning, Michael found a note under the door. It was made with the hotel stationary and read, "IT PAYS TO VOLUNTEER -D." Donahue's plan was in motion, though Michael had no idea what he should volunteer for. To be a walker again? Could that kind of selflessness show that he deserved a spot on the wagons? Or maybe they needed someone to do some damage. His pink rifle was silly, but it was known around camp that he knew how to use it. He made his way to the mess tent to get his morning portion when he noticed a crowd gathered at the other end. Joe was calling everyone in and there was a man on his knees with a burlap sack over his head. Michael went over, wondering if they needed a volunteer executioner.

"Citizens, we are embroiled in controversy this morning. I know you'd rather be eating and preparing and relaxing, but this matter is too important to save for any time other than right now. This," he stumbled, searching for words, "man… This thing, is a traitor to this group, to the republic, and to all the virtues that we promote as a species. Last night, our friend here was tasked with guarding us as we slept. His duty to protect our lives at the risk of his own is such an important and noble endeavor, that special privileges were deemed acceptable. He would get a slightly larger meal portion, he was excused from the harder jobs around camp. When we were on the road, he got to ride in the main wagon with a little extra room to catch some sleep before that night's watch. And he took advantage of every bit of it. So last night, when he should have been repaying us for our generosity and understanding, instead, he was asleep, dozed off dreaming of other ways to screw us."

"It's not true. I don't know what happened. I must have fallen and hit my head. I swear, I didn't mean to fall asleep," the man cried.

"Quiet!" he yelled. "Don't fall for his lies, Citizens. I couldn't believe it myself until I saw him, perched under a tree, legs crossed and oh so comfortable. One of our fellow citizens alerted me and had enough civic discipline to take the rest of the watch for us, even though he'd done more than his fair share until that point. So, I leave it to you to decide his fate, dear Citizens. Should he be banished or made an example of?"

There was murmuring in the crowd. Joe knew how to stir up a mob and after some grumbling, it didn't take much for them to start calling for his head. Joe had been the one who kept them safe thus far. He was the one who warned them about the drones and provided protection. Every move he made was right in their eyes and they wanted to repay him for his magnanimity.

"He died last night when he fell asleep, Joe" one called out.

"If we let him live, it might come back and bite us in the ass."

"He needs to be made an example!"

Joe cracked a slight smile. The man in the bag was crying, begging for banishment, in between wails of innocence.

"Very well. Jose, dispatch the traitor."

Jose walked up and put the barrel of his rifle up against the back of the man's head, where the brain met the spine. He fired a single shot from the bolt action hunting rifle and it rang out far and wide. The bullet shredded the head, exited the bag, and spilled bits of blood and brain all over the ground. Jose turned towards camp, getting first in line for their morning portion of slop. The body was to stay as is. No funeral. No eulogy. No grave.

"I'll need a volunteer to take over for the traitor. Someone reliable, who will put the needs of the Republic above his own creature comforts. Anyone?"

The mood of the crowd shifted as the weight of it all set in. Now there was a precedence. Anyone who fucks up was sure to die. Just like that man, who didn't even get a name or last words. The energy of the crowd was sapped away and Michael saw the same men who called for death, now staring at the floor, shuffling around in discomfort. It pays to volunteer and just like that, Michael raised his hand high in the air.

"I'll do it," he announced. "I'll watch over the group. Keep us safe at night."

There were a few sighs of relief and Joe smiled wide. "Citizen Connors, you have impressed me. I don't often change my opinions, but the last day has revealed your sense of duty. I've never been so happy to be wrong before. Get some breakfast and then take the day to rest and prepare. You start tonight."

A few people patted Michael on the shoulder, gave him words of encouragement, and then moved to get in line for breakfast. Michael was pushed to the front and got a more substantial portion than he'd grown used to, as well as a few pieces of beef jerky. As he sat down to eat, he saw Donahue, who gave him a nod. Michael returned it and went back to his plate.

CHAPTER TEN

Two months had passed since Michael left Jersey City and the strife aged him several years. A patchy beard grew on his face of differing lengths, longer on the neck and cheeks, but thinner closer to his jaw. The muscle he'd built over the years was leaving him, feasted upon by his body as finding and securing proper nourishment became more and more difficult. They were near Iowa now and since he'd become the night guard, he grew more and more distant. Meanwhile, Donahue was charming them, telling made-up stories about his life as a stockbroker in New York before the war. He sang vulgar songs and played a beat-up guitar, entertaining the group all evening.

Every night, Michael was on watch. Every morning, he pretended to sleep in the back of one of the wagons. He ate alone after everyone else had eaten. He washed alone, still trying to figure out the words that would set him free. He knew they were wary of him and would kill him if he gave them enough cause. He was close to dead in Gary. He wouldn't repeat his mistakes.

The solitude gave Michael time to try and remember things. Phrases, memories, anything to figure out what he said that shut him off from his humanity. He could remember rolling down

143

the hall in a gurney at the base hospital. The floors had just been cleaned and smelled like Mop & Glo. A maintenance man was repairing a broken light further down. The room number was 409, his sister's birthday. When the doctor asked him if he'd eaten, Michael replied, 'No, Sir' even though the doctor wasn't in the military. He didn't wear a stethoscope and a large orderly strapped him down to a table, then gave him knockout gas, which frightened him. He was told he'd be awake for the surgery, that brain surgery was dangerous and they needed to ask him questions while they worked.

But he woke up fine and alert and felt the same as before he'd gone under. A different doctor tested his cognition and was typing away at a computer as they spoke. She had kind eyes, though they looked on him with sadness. She had short, black hair and looked like she listened to alt-rock. She was the last woman he'd ever been attracted to, but he couldn't recall her name. In his memory, he tried to recall the badge on her lab coat, 'Dr. Something', it read. He could hear her asking if he was ready to choose a trigger phrase.

"Make it something personal. Something you could never forget,"

He felt a push on his shoulder, a small hand wringing back and forth, trying to get his attention. It was the runt, Peter, who'd always attracted the ire of the other boys. He was small for his age, too skinny, and looked sickly. When food was going around, he was always given double portions, but it did no use. Michael was sure the boy would die before they got to California, though he kept that opinion to himself.

"What?" Michael snarled.

"Hi! I'm Peter," he replied, oblivious to Michael's surliness.

"What can I do for you, Peter?" he asked, accentuating his annoyance.

"I've met everyone already, except you. I have to meet everyone in the group before Matt does and then I win."

"Win what?"

The boy shrugged. It'd been a long time since Michael had played a game, let alone one that had no clear stakes except for the pride that one gets from winning. But the boy shouldn't have been so far from the others, especially as it was getting darker.

"Why don't you ask Mr. Donahue about me. I'm sure he'd tell you."

"Mom says we can't talk to Mr. Donahue. Plus, he looks weird. He's always staring at people. He only really talks to Cherry. I asked her if he was her boyfriend cause I saw them kissing a couple times, but she said no and laughed."

"It's probably best you listen to your mother, then."

"Mom's not my real Mom. She just told me to call her that. My real mom is…" he trailed off and looked to the ground.

That small amount of empathy that he had, which he nicknamed the pity protocol, kicked in. He put his hand on the boy's shoulder and gave him a squeeze. The boy then wrapped

145

his arms around Michael's forearm. He resisted the urge to shake the boy loose and instead stayed there until he was ready to let go.

"What do you want to know?" Michael asked, trying to cheer him up. Peter let go and grabbed a small notepad and a golf pencil he had stuck out of the spiral. Michael could see the small notes he'd made and noticed he had good handwriting for a boy his age, though he admitted to himself that he was unsure how old Peter even was.

"What is your full name? Mom says you're Mr. Connors, but what's your first name? And your middle name?"

"Michael. Michael Alan Connors"

"Why are you going to California?"

Michael thought about that one. He and Donahue decided early on to act like they didn't know each other. It was easier that way.

"I'm going to see my Sister," he replied.

"Oh, okay." The boy scribbled something down in the notepad.

"How come Mr. Abe doesn't like you?"

Abe was an Amish farmer they'd met in Cleveland. He kept mostly to himself and his wife, Prudence, was the more social, though it was a marginal difference. He was a middle-aged man, probably in his late forties, early fifties. He seldom said much of anything, but Michael noticed that he kept a flask on his person and visited him frequently. He wanted to ask for a drink one day but decided it was probably best to not poke the old bear. Ever since Michael arrived in Cleveland, he felt Abe's staring, like a searchlight on escaped convicts.

"I don't know. I don't talk to him often. What did he say?"

"He just said I shouldn't ask you questions. And that it's best if me and Matt stayed away from you, too."

The sun had set already and dinner was about to be served. There was no doubt that the others would be looking for Peter and that he probably couldn't get all the way back to the campsite on his own in the dark. Michael took the boy's hand and walked him back to the others, where he found Matt and gloated that he'd won the game. Matt started pouting until the next game was announced and they started throwing rocks as far out into the dark as they could.

"Mr. Connors," the boy's mother, the same woman who'd been serving the meals started, "Why don't you join us around the fire for supper?"

Michael usually sneaked in and out while they were eating to get his plate and leave. "Mom" as she liked to be called, always left enough for him. He knew he already had so much suspicion around him and decided to appease her, if only for one night. He took his plate and stood in line behind Donahue, who was playing grab-ass with one of the new pick-ups, Cherry, in front of him. The Amish couple had already taken a seat and Werner stood behind Michael, followed by Anne, and finally, Joe, who declared that leaders should always eat last.

"Gut Evening, Herr Michael, it feels like so long since we have seen you at dinner," said Werner, keeping up his appearances with the others.

"Evening," Michael replied.

"Citizen Connors understands his role in this caravan," Joe piped in. "He does his job without complaint and will be a model citizen in the Pacific States Republic. We can all learn from his example."

Anne rolled her eyes and gave him a yes, dear kind of response. The line moved quickly and they were soon all around the fire. Michael was between the burly, yet soft-hearted Mom and Donahue, who was keeping his attention fully fixed on Cherry, who they'd picked up in Gary. The dinner was quiet until Werner brought out a large bottle of schnapps. He passed it around the fire, first to Mom, who smelled it and took a small sip, then wiped the rim with her shirt. Michael took a good sip and passed it without a word.

"Where the hell did you get this anyway," Donahue asked after taking a swig.

"A shopkeeper we met in Gary. His mother was Austrian and he gave me the bottle as a gift. He was a very kind person. He asked for nothing in return, which was good because I had nothing to give him. I tried to give him a picture of the Danube near Linz that I kept in my wallet, but he refused." Michael knew it was bullshit. "Werner" found that sack of potatoes and traded it for the hooch first chance he got. He was a first-class scrounger.

"It's good," Cherry added. Michael knew very little of Donahue's paramour. She looked like she'd always been skinny, her arms covered in tattoos and a pair of fake tits that were more pronounced now that she was perpetually hungry. He remembered the man outside of the Gracie back in Jersey. He remembered the beating Donahue had given that man. He worried Donahue would do the same to her, not for any concern towards her well-being, but because he wasn't sure they could make it all the way without the safety that numbers brought. And he wasn't sure he could make it without Donahue, which he found hardest to swallow.

The bottle was half-finished when it got to Prudence, who politely declined as Abe reached over and took it from her. He gave Werner a furious look.

"We were in Gary three weeks, ago. Why'd you hold out this long?"

"I was keeping it for a special occasion. Herr Michael has never joined us for dinner, I thought it required some libations."

Abe took the bottle and drank the rest of it, much to the annoyance of Anne, who hadn't yet gotten any. He let the empty bottle fall to the ground and let out a small belch. Anne looked to Prudence, who tried to ignore her husband's boorish behavior. When nothing happened, Anne raised her hand to slap him in the back of the head, only for Joe to stop her.

"What the fuck was that for, Abe?"

"I was thirsty."

"You're a drunk, is what you are. I never heard of a Drunken Amish."

"There are no more Amish," he replied. "Mr. Connors over there saw to that, didn't you? You and your soulless, devil-men. You came in and took our boy from us. Him and every other man to fight in your pestilential war."

They all looked at Michael, hoping he'd clear up the confusion.

"I don't know what he's talking about. The first time I'd met you was on the road, same as everyone else."

"Aye," Prudence answered, "but you know what he means, don't you? You know where my boy is right now. You must tell us, Sir, please!"

Michael felt like his cover had been blown. Somehow the old man or his wife had known that he was a recruiter. He'd been so careful to keep his distance and in the span of a half-hour, he'd been sussed out like a snake in a garden. All eyes were upon him, even Donahue, who was just keeping up appearances. It was the contingency he'd dreaded since the start, to be lynched in the middle of nowhere by those he once bonded into servitude.

"Why don't you take us from the beginning, Citizen Prudence," Joe suggested. "Give us all a clearer picture of what you're talking about."

"I can do it," Abe hollered. "It all started over a little five years ago. When your electricity and your godless technology failed you all, you were all freed from its influence and you could have rejoiced at your liberation. But you panicked instead. We had a store in Lancaster that we had to shut down. Too much looting and violence after a few months of peace and law and order. Lots of soldiers walking around until they weren't anymore. Then we started seeing things go missing. Some food from the granary. Clothes from lines. Whole crops pulled out of the ground. People sleeping in our barns. We welcomed many as newcomers but told them that they'd have to adapt to our way of life. Hard work from dawn til dusk. Prayer on the Sabbath. Learn how to read Dutch. Some did. Many didn't. Soon, the number of English outweighed the Amish and they brought their culture and their idle hands with them. Many women didn't want to keep homes. Most of the men were useless on the land. Soon enough, people started to leave when food was running low. We weren't even sure how we'd last the winter, but my great-great-grandfather had built our home. I wouldn't abandon my birthright so easily."

Abe took out his flask and took a long swig. Prudence looked at him with tears in her eyes. The others were enticed by the story, even the boys, who seemed to not fully grasp what they were hearing. He wiped his mouth and continued.

"We did what we always did when things got tough. We got tough. We prayed to God. We put our destiny in our own hands and though we suffered, we survived that first, dreadful winter. We were half what we'd once been by the end of it. We thought the worst would be over. Then, a couple of months ago, a pack of Devil-Men came to us, having no soul in their eyes. They told us that all the men were to come with them and that they were drafted into an army. My father had been drafted to go to Vietnam, but we Amish could choose to not go. We are pacifists. Conscientious objectors, they called us. God-fearing men, we called it. We thought that this was the same thing and told them to leave, that we weren't fighting any war as we had in the past."

He pulled another long swig as drops of the whiskey missed his mouth and spilled in droplets onto his trousers.

"They got angry and started beating on the old men and women. Stealing the youth from our community and shoving them into the backs of their trucks like cattle to the slaughter. They burned down my house and all the houses around us. Killed anyone who got in their way. Urinated and defecated where they pleased. Violated the women. By the end of it, when they left, there weren't many of us still standing. Soon, it was just Prudence and I. And eventually, we left, too. I thought I would die there, but God had different plans for us."

Prudence started rubbing a small bump in her mid-section. She was probably in her early forties while Abe was at least ten years her senior.

"And you think that Citizen Connors was one of the men who did this?"

"No, he wasn't there," Abe spewed, "But he's one of 'em. Look in those eyes. Alert, like a beast. Cornered. Caught."

They all looked over to Michael, scanning his eyes with great interest. They were a soft, sullen blue. As they stared at him, he was looking at the fire, the flames flickering in those blue portals to a soul that was locked away. After a while, they stopped staring. None knew what Abe knew, which Michael found even more curious.

"Mr. Donahue, you traveled with him before any of us. What do you think?" Anne asked.

"He was quiet. I asked him where he was going and if he wanted company. He didn't answer, but he didn't say know. I don't know him better than I know any of you. But he looked like someone who could handle himself and I figured it was better to be around someone like that out here."

"Well, that doesn't mean anything," Werner replied.

"It could mean he's a Rep!" Cherry countered.

"It could mean anything!" Werner replied. "I've lived with Herr Michael for most of the journey and I can tell you, not once have I seen anything suspicious from him. He is quiet, yes. Keeps to himself, but in this harsh world, who is not wary of others? Your very suspicions prove that he is right to be that way."

"I'll make it simple for everyone," Michael chimed in, "If you think I can't be trusted, I'll leave. I can make better time to the West Coast on my own. I'd rather take my life into my own hands than to wait to be executed and left to rot where I fall." Michael finished the rest of his plate and threw it down onto the ground. "Funny how I never seem to hear these accusations when the sun rises."

Michael grabbed his rifle, which by now had been covered in different dark fabrics and camouflages, which Michael found more than agreeable. The others continued debating and Joe, who looked bored with the whole ordeal, changed the subject.

"Citizens, wouldn't you rather know more about how to live in our Republic? Life there is so much different than what you are accustomed to. Take, driving a car, for instance. Behind the frontlines, cars can be purchased by a household, so long as there are enough members of a household to fit the vehicle. Carpooling is mandatory and you'll be levied a hefty fine if you're caught with a less than full vehicle." He trailed off as Michael stomped further from the fire pit. Earlier in the day, he spotted a thick group of overgrown shrubs on a higher section of the highway median that would provide a good amount of visibility. He'd gotten six hours of sleep in the last two weeks.

The night was quiet and Michael looked up in the sky and counted stars to pass the time. Previous nights, he'd gotten a few hundred before giving up. From time to time, he'd spot a drone flying overhead. Most of the older models, ones that had the old regulation blinking lights had been shot down already, so Michael could only really see then as they obscured the shimmering starlight above him. The one good thing about the ETPs was that they worked. His heightened focus could see most things in the clearest detail. Motion seemed slower, sounds were crisper and louder, color more vivid, even at night time, and taste more acute. Now more than ever, could his tastebuds appreciate the works of the world's finest chefs and his eyes, the most dazzling art, but those sensations were otherwise wasted except that he could identify ingredients and find waldo a lot faster than before. In between bouts with the heavenly lights, Michael tried remembering. Another benefit of the ETPs, he could do the same thing over and over again without losing an ounce of sanity. He went through the list of crushes he had in high school, this time. If it were one of them and it worked, he promised to slap himself, hard. None of the names caused any stir and for all his heightened senses, he was too late when he felt the barrel of a rifle square against his back.

"You were sleeping," Jose accused.

"I wasn't."

"You were. I could hear you muttering some girl's names. Dreaming about old girlfriends, Amigo?"

"I was…" he began to rationalize. "I was awake, that's all you need to know."

"If you were awake, how did I get the drop on you, huh? What good is a nightguard if someone can sneak up on him so easily."

"I was wondering that myself. Not many could do that without me hearing."

"Ah, so then I think we both know the answer, but don't want to admit it."

"What do you mean?" Michael said, confused and uncertain. "If you're going to shoot me, just do it. I've never liked when this shit was dragged out. Just do it and get it over with."

"I know what you are, Pendejo," Jose whispered. "Ask me how I know. Go ahead, ask me." But he didn't have to.

155

"You're a Rep."

"No, but you are. I'm a United States Marine. Well, I was. Now, I'm just a lost soul, in a living purgatory. Have you started getting the headaches yet?"

"Headaches?"

"I get such bad ones when I don't sleep for too long. Longest bout was three months. The migraines were so painful, only thing that helped was morphine."

"I used Ambien for a while. That and liquor."

"Word of advice. Don't use MDMA. I knew a guy who popped Molly to get the feeling back. He kept having to up the dosage because the computer got smarter and smarter, balancing him out every time he tried to take the same amount. Then, his body couldn't take anymore. Braindead."

The rifle was still in Michael's back and Jose made a point of letting him remember with a couple of soft jabs. Michael was too interested to fight, however. It was a Remington 700 bolt action rifle. Matte Black with bits of rust that any drill sergeant would mark a failure from fifty yards out. It had no long-range scope, but instead a set of iron sights.

"Why don't you put the gun down? This is the first time I've met someone like… me."

"Sure thing, after a few more questions. Why are you here? Why are you moving out West? And don't give me that shit about your sister. Are you a scout? Is the invasion coming soon?"

"If I could laugh… There ain't gonna be an invasion any time soon, Bud. Trust me."

"I'd like to, but thus far, you've appeared less than trustworthy."

"When I left, they were ramping up to take New York."

"Yeah right, they took New York right after DC. That was two years ago. They've got to be down the East Coast by now and moving West."

"Nope. We bypassed most of the East Coast cities moving down to Florida. Baltimore, DC, NYC are all outside Deluge's domain. Don't even get me started on the South. It's a clusterfuck."

"Well, at least some things don't change. Water's wet, shit smells, and the news lies."

Michael had no choice but to come clean. Jose would know a lie and if his stealth were an indicator, it was doubtful Michael would win in a fight.

"I'm on a sort of bounty. I've been sent to go knock off a scientist. Alex Mercer asked me personally."

"The Oedipal King himself, no shit. One of the PSR's scientists?"

"No, he's hiding out."

"He got a name?"

"Not one I'm telling. I don't need you trying to rescue him."

"Not my game. Though I wouldn't tell Joe. Guy will do anything to curry favor."

"I didn't even want to tell you, but" he nudged his back into the barrel of the rifle, "present circumstances kinda threw that plan out."

"One more question. That other guy, Donahue, he's also a Rep? He on the same mission?"

"You're sharp, Jose. I'll give you that."

"When Donahue knocked out the last guard, I thought it odd."

"Why not tell Joe?"

Jose shrugged his shoulders and lowered the rifle. For a second, Michael thought about trying to take him out. Second thoughts and better judgment prevented that mistake and the two took a seat by the shrubs. While Michael did not enjoy things, it was the closest he'd come in some time. Jose had some hooch, but Michael declined. Besides the Schnapps, he hadn't had a drink since Cleveland and he wanted to see if that could stir anything. Michael looked back up at the night's sky and blurted out the first thing that came to mind.

"I've counted six hundred and eighty-five different stars." He left it there, waiting to see what Jose would say in return. He looked up in the sky and gazed at them as well.

"There's this old joke about these two prisoners. One's been in for ten years and the other, twenty. The ten-year guy says, 'I've counted all five thousand, four hundred, and sixty-eight stones that make up this prison cell at least a hundred times.' The twenty-year guy goes, 'Yeah, but have you named them all yet?'"

"That's funny," Michael said in a tone far from laughter.

"It helps to make jokes. Even if you don't understand them. People will laugh. Especially dark jokes. They think you staying stone-faced is part of it. Give it a try. It'll keep eyes off your back. Or don't, then one day Joe might tell me to shoot you and I will."

They were quiet for a while. Michael heard no pleasure in Jose's voice. No malice in his promise that he would shoot Michael as soon as ordered. There wasn't even boredom like some people have when describing how they took out the trash or how their lunch was. Instead, it was confident, matter of fact. Michael could appreciate that.

"How'd it happen to you? Knock on the head? Doesn't look like it was a bullet," Jose asked.

"IED. Explosion knocked me back like a rag doll and when I came to, I couldn't remember how to come back home. You?"

"Yeah, meat cleaver of all things. Dude came at me like an old-timey butcher while I was taking out his buddy and he swung and cut just right. One in a million shot."

"What did you do from there?"

"I turned around and shot him in the face. He looked so spooked, he started backing up and muttering about how I was the devil or something. I don't know, I don't speak Farsi. I still had the thing in my head and I got a lot of weird looks when I came out of the shop. Corpsman asked me to turn off to judge if I had pain and I said, 'When life itself seems lunatic, who knows where madness lies?' and nothing happened. I tried it again. And then again. And again, like I was trying to fix my computer. Nada."

Jose looked off into the distance.

"Not a day goes by that I wish he hadn't killed me."

"Why keep it up then? If you don't want to do it yourself, I could even-"

"I still have the smallest bit of hope."

A few more hours passed and the sun was beginning to peak through the hills and the sky was aglow with warm colors, chasing out the night's darkness. Today was the Solstice and the caravan would take advantage of every second of light. Jose left the post with Michael following ten minutes later. He hadn't had hope before, but the slim chance that Jose gave himself filled Michael with possibility. It was dangerous to hope, even a little. But he could permit it that morning. Even he could recognize a beautiful sunrise.

CHAPTER ELEVEN

Michael was standing in a field of tall grass, his mother's face was the sun and toward the horizon, a female shape that got no clearer the closer he moved. The individual blades of grass whispered to him different words and phrases. One was a song and others were things his father told him. Mrs. Horcheimer's voice shrilled about a missing assignment and Rutger Hauer lamented about tears in rain.

"Connors? Your Bitch ass still alive?" Sergeant Ross called to him.

"Yeah, Sarge. I'm okay."

Sergeant Ross was laying in the grass, his uniform ripped to shreds. The grass was drenched red in blood around him and the air grew thick with dust.

"Didn't think I'd go like this," he whispered. A large earthquake started breaking up the ground and the grass fell in between the cracks. Michael reached out for Ross but couldn't move his arms and saw the man fall deep down to the unknown below. He sat up in the back of the wagon, flailing his arms, his eyes barely open.

"Fuck me," he whispered. It was the first dream he could remember in quite some time. In the distance, he heard the distinct sounds of civilization and the cacophony of business, leisure, and everything in between. He hopped out of the wagon and saw all kinds of PSR flags and uniformed personnel walking around. Interspersed were townsfolk and merchants and at their shops were other migrants like himself. The sign on the outskirts said Bridgeton and behind the shanties, shacks, and temporary structures was a wide, river-spanning tension bridge that had been blown up, its metal beams twisted about and jutting off into all different directions.

"Michael!" Peter shouted, running over to greet him. "You were having a bad dream. Mom said I shouldn't wake you up, but you were screaming and moving around. Are you okay?"

"Fine. Thanks."

"I used to have bad dreams all the time. When we were in my old house, my real mom used to cry a lot, and sometimes, I would dream that she was crying."

"You're a very open person, you know that," Michael commented, the critique going right over the child's head. The boy beamed a bright smile and ran off, elated with childhood zeal. John, the old hippie, was watching him and cackling his familiar laugh, needing staples to keep his sides from splitting further. He was playing chess with the other old man, Bobby. The small, white cat was crawling on the ground, stalking a mouse that Michael had noticed scurrying out of the corner of his eye. Bobby was in check and grumbled about wanting to switch back to checkers.

"Something funny?"

"You know, for a hard son of a gun, you've got a soft spot for that boy."

"Yup, I'm a real humanitarian."

The old man cackled again and moved a rook across the board, putting Bobby back in check. Bobby moved a pawn, only for it to be swiped away. John's cool demeanor and grating laugh only frustrated the geezer more and more. He stood up and shouted, "Listen, Garry Kasparov, after this game, we're switching to cards. We'll deal this kid in and I'll be wearing your sandals faster than you can say Woodstock." As he yelled, a small can of cat food flew out of his pocket and rolled on the grass below. He jumped on the can like it were made of gold and shoved it back into his pocket. John pretended not to see and Michael grew curious.

"I'll give you a couple if you don't say anything. Deal?"

"Tempting, but I don't have a cat."

This launched them both into a hysteric fit, so loud and boisterous, they almost knocked the board over. Bobby almost started crying and after five minutes of unending mirth, they settled down, wiping the tears from their eyes and the snot from their noses.

"Boy, you're a trip, you know that?"

"He doesn't know," said Bobby. "Felicia was an outdoor cat her whole life. She hunts for her meals. But this", he said, holding the small can of meat, "This is the last solid food source that people always seem to overlook."

He popped open the lid and grabbed a small fork he had stowed in the same pocket and scarfed down the small tin of wet food, making sure to drink up the leftover juices before sticking the cleaned-out can back in his pocket. He offered one to John, who took it and did the same, then looked to Michael to see if he wanted one as well. He stuck his hand out and shook his head.

"People will eat Chef Boyardee no problem, but wince at Friskies. I don't get it. Smells the same to me. It's cooked. It lasts for a while. Hell, I saw some organic stuff that you'd have thought was meant for people."

"Tastes better than the shit we ate in Nam, that's for sure," John added.

"You were in Vietnam, old man?" Michael asked.

"Indeed. 101st Airborne. Spent most of my year in the A Shau valley. Made all this look like kindergarten."

He laughed a bit and Michael laughed, too. Bobby laughed for a second, but shifted gears not long after and stared at the can of cat food in his hands.

"Best we leave the past behind us, eh?" Bobby shot, eyeing up John with a glare that could freeze molten rock. They sat in awkward silence for what felt like an eternity. It had been over sixty years since the last choppers left Saigon, but Michael would have thought Bobby had just come home. The wounds were fresh it seemed.

"Greatest gee-tarist ever, go?" John demanded and just like that, his titanic charisma swept away the mood like a monsoon.

"Oh, not this again. You know my answer."

"Indulge me. For the kid's sake."

Michael was unused to being called a kid but minded it less and less as it went on. It reminded him of when his father played cards in the dining room and he'd let Michael play a few hands every once in a while. He remembered being happy then.

"Hendrix. No question. He makes another album, he's enshrined forever. But because he was so great, the music gods had to take him in his prime."

John wagged his finger and laughed. "Ah, ah, ah. There is one gee-tarist that's head and shoulders above any musician ever. Even Beethoven woulda bowed to this guy. And you know who that is?"

Bobby rolled his eyes and said, "Mark Knopfler."

"Mark. Knopfler. Greatest musician ever. Totally underappreciated by his contemporaries and all but forgotten by those who came after who shoulda been kissing his feet. If he died at twenty-seven, there would be monuments to the man. But he had the fortitude to stick around."

Michael smiled to be polite but found it taxing like he was turning old gears whose rust fused them together. It looked just as unnatural and he ended the gesture before the geezers noticed. They were too busy to see anything but what was in front of them.

"Jim Morrison was an artist. He was a poet. Up there with his contemporaries. Dylan got the Nobel prize, Morrison could have, too."

"Oh please, Shakespeare, explain the lyrical genius of Touch Me."

Bobby huffed. "Better than 'Come Dancing." He grabbed a deck of cards from his pack as Bobby cleared their makeshift table.

"You know how to play Rummy, Kid?"

Michael shook his head and watched the two men play a few hands and picked up the game quick. They played to five hundred points. He ended with three hundred and twenty-five. They shuffled up again and kept the game going for some time.

"I was just listening to Springsteen the other day. I don't care what you say, but the Boss knows, man. He fucking knows."

"How'd you do that?" Michael asked. "He on this highway to hell, too?" he joked.

John and Bobby looked at one another and Bobby spun his head in every direction. John put out his hand and beckoned Michael in as he opened the flap of his thin, ratty jacket. John reached in the inner pocket and produced an old iPod, the first generation with the small screen and over one hundred gigabytes of storage. It was dented, cracked, discolored, and looked like it would explode if turned on, but when John stuck one of the earbuds in Michael's ear, he heard the piercing screech of Brian Johnson's Aussie bellow on the track of "Hells Bells" and he was transported back to his childhood, his father driving their beat-up Dodge Neon like it were a Charger, tapping on the steering wheel to the beat while Michael could only try and sing along, but knowing none of the words.

"Ain't that some shit, Kid?" Bobby smiled, patting him on the back. "You said Highway to Hell, didn't ya?"

"My dad loved AC/DC."

"Course he did. Every man does. Don't matter that it's basically the same damn song over and over again. It's a good goddamn song."

Michael noticed the battery was at fifteen percent and he knew those old iPods could keep charged forever. He guessed that the old man had been listening since May Day.

"The trick is to listen sparingly. Only when I get the itch. But, I'm like an old junkie. I need the fix more and more. My last birthday I listened to the whole of "Darkside of the Moon" as a treat to myself. I figure I'll listen to Brother's in Arms by my next one. Sooner if we get to California before then."

"When's your Birthday?" Michael asked without enthusiasm like disgruntled cashiers ask if someone wants fries with that.

"June Nineteenth. PSR federal Holiday, too. Not sure why."

"Juneteenth," Bobby replied. "June Nineteenth, 1865. The day the last slaves were freed in America."

"Oh, well how about that?" John answered. "How the hell you know that, Bobby?"

"Guy in my wing went on and on about it. Black Power movement was all over every inch of the Vietnam war. It was like a war within the war."

"You were in Vietnam, too?" Michael asked with the innocence and ignorance of a slow child. In his mind, he was beating himself up for such stupidity. Outside, he kept his eyes on Bobby.

"I was in the Air Force," Bobby added. His demeanor changed and the once jovial, if not a little unhinged, old man grew hard and cold. "I flew missions out of Bien Hoa. They didn't tell us what we were messing with. I never had to worry about dropping bombs on the wrong guys or civilians. I know guys that had. There are few worse sins than that."

His hand began to fidget as if it were holding a cigarette that he seemed desperate for. "They told me it was some kind of plant killer. Then," he stopped, composing himself, there were tears welling up in the corners of his eyes, "all these years later, Agent Orange becomes synonymous with Zyklon-B. I remember my Pilot, Captain Jennings, say 'Oops' over the radio when some grunts called in and complained that they got doused in that shit because we missed the target. I thought Jennings was a good guy. Party boy type. Wine, Women, and all

169

that shit. The wing met up years later, after rumors and reports and exposes. And that good time guy just sat there, getting piss drunk, denying what was so obvious. He died not long after. Cancer. Most of the guys died that way. We killed more people than the gooks ever did. And we did it in a far worse way. And here I am, healthy as an ox. An old ox, sure, but healthy. There it fucking is."

It was quiet for a long time. Bobby just looked out into the distance, at nothing in particular. Michael took stock of the man and if he could like people, Bobby would be someone he liked. John put his hand on Bobby's shoulder. Michael was unsure what was said, but knew the small gesture communicated more than any cliched phrases ever could. John squeezed Bobby's shoulder blade tight and Bobby just put his hand on John's, who didn't let go. Michael wanted to talk about his experiences. His war. Sergeant Ross. But he wasn't a soldier. Not now, not to them. That was too many red flags. Maybe he could trust these men. They understood, didn't they? Good soldiers follow orders. He could tell them everything and they'd understand. They'd keep it quiet. And not out of fear, like Werner, but out of understanding. Because they knew what it was. He could tell them about the murder houses and the dead and the soon-to-be-dead. He could tell them about recruiting. But then, Michael came back to cold reality. He couldn't. These men were drafted, most likely. And if they weren't, they knew someone who was. Someone who probably didn't make it home. Another bit of meat for the machine to grind out. He'd keep quiet and nod and try to pretend that he had no idea what they were talking about.

They played cards for a while until it was time to eat and Michael would go on watch for the evening. They had a special meal that night, courtesy of the outpost's canteen. Canned pork and beans with some stale bread to sop up the remaining juices. The small styrofoam bowl represented the most substantial meal he'd had since leaving New Jersey. He ate next to the old men and the cat, who hadn't stirred from her nap the whole evening. The two old men laughed and kidded each other, while Michael acted as more of a fly on the wall than a participant. It was nice, he thought. Normal. He was being normal.

When he finished, Michael gathered his gear and headed off to his post. He thanked the old men for the meal and thought about petting the cat, but she looked too content to be disturbed, so he didn't. He went to the town security office to get an assignment. It was the first time that he'd only be responsible for a small sector instead of the entire perimeter, and he welcomed the break. As he approached the security office, he passed the canteen. It was the first building he'd seen with lights on since leaving New Jersey and the music bumped and thumped so loud that Michael felt it in his chest. He decided his post could wait for a second and entered the party, beelining straight for the bar. The bartender, a portly man that looked like he'd fit in at any old western saloon, dressed in heavy cotton that was sun-bleached and covered in loose threads, sized Michael up and down and without a word spoken, poured three fingers of whiskey into a glass and sat it in front of the man. The bartender, his arms crossed, wearing a satisfied smug, waited for Michael to pick up the glass as if to say, "I pegged you as soon as you walked in." Michael raised his glass to his omniscient server and drained the glass in a single, smooth motion. The bartender went to pour another but Michael waved him off, content to stand and admire the scene before him.

The canteen was full of people from the caravan. Abe was at the other end of the bar, resting his head on the wooden bar top, his last shot of rye spilled all over him. Donahue was entertaining Cherry, who, sitting on his lap, whispered something into his ear before he threw her off of him, grabbed her by the arm, and forced the crowd to make way as they stormed out in a fury, the both of them grinning. Donahue noticed Michael at the bar and gave him a knowing wink, which Michael saw, but chose not to acknowledge. About to leave, Michael noticed that Joe was sitting in the corner, drinking alone, and glaring at Anne, who seemed quite popular with the other men of the PSR. Michael tipped his no existent cap to Joe, who answered by finishing his drink, wiping his mouth with his arm, and moving to the bartender for another. Michael turned and left to take his post.

Michael reached the security office and was met by the town's security officer, Major Stenka. He was a lean, tall drink of water, who shaved every hair on his head except his eyebrows and lashes, though upon further inspection it seemed even the brows weren't safe from his razor's fury, as a gap between the left and right brow indicated that he shaved the middle, preventing an unsightly unibrow from taking hold of his otherwise mediocre face.

"You Joe's guy?" Stenka asked.

"Yeah," Michael replied.

"Soldiers reply 'Yes Sir' around here," replied Stenka. Several of the PSR soldiers in the office stopped what they were doing to listen in on the ass-chewing that Stenka was about to dole out.

"Well, it's a good thing I'm not a Soldier. Otherwise, you'd have to shoot me for having a drink right before my watch, too."

"You're a civilian? That fucking figures. What happened to Joe's body man? Santos. Where the fuck is he?"

"No idea."

Stenka could only sit behind his desk and shuffle papers like he was interrogating them for information. He gave Michael the Easternmost sector, which also happened to be the widest one. It was clear Michael did himself no favors by mouthing off, but he figured Stenka started it by being an asshole and only returned the favor. Michael left the building and on his way to his post, noticed a small SAM battery on the outskirts of the town. The loud music, still blaring, was rendered quiet by the blast from the battery's rocket, which flew up into the sky at great speed and hit an unseen object far off in the distance. The soldiers around the battery, acting from what looked like routine, worked to reload the missile system and then went back to the monotony that was their daily life. The music regained its place as the loudest noise in the area. Michael took his post and watched as the sun shrunk off in the distance. A few hours in, Jose arrived for their nightly rendezvous. They walked Michael's post like good sentries, talking and bullshitting the whole time, sure that nothing in the air or on the ground was coming after them that night.

"That Major asked about you. Wondered why you weren't the one on watch."

"Who? Stenka? He a major now?"

"Yup, gold oakleaf on the color. Not a hair on his dome nor a thought inside it as far as I could tell."

"He's alright."

"He's an asshole."

"He was my platoon leader."

"No shit?"

"Yup. 1st Platoon, Lima Company 3rd Battalion 1st Marines."

"You didn't tell me you were 3/1."

"Didn't know you knew any difference."

"I was in the Third Infantry Battalion. You guys were on our flanks on the push to Tehran."

"That was heavy shit. Not Pendleton, but pretty fucking heavy."

He'd known from reputation that 3/1's push into Tehran was a shit show. From the moment they landed at Bushehr, they slogged across an ungodly, mountainous terrain. When they reached Qom, it was 3/1 that went in first. Four times, they were pushed out of the city. Four times, Twelver radicals drove VBIEDs right into the convoys, as if the lessons from Iraq had never quite sunk into American doctrine.

"What happened at Pendleton?" Michael asked with intrigue and slight apprehension. Military culture was built into two hierarchies. The ranking of individuals provided the obvious pecking order of officer and enlisted, senior mentors, and their junior, green pupils. In between the obvious, existed a gray area that all officers and enlisted measured each other against. A hierarchy of hardships granted respect to those who went to the deepest depths of hell and came back, compared to those whose more shallow experiences subordinated them to the veterans of Pandemonium.

"When the PSR took control, they ordered all the military bases to surrender and pledge their allegiance. I'd been out for some time but figured there was no other way for me to make a living, so I joined their security forces. I figured the majority of the guys on base would ask to be let out of their contracts and go back to wherever they came from or even maybe sign up and fight for the PSR. That's what the word on the street was at least. Well, that sure as shit didn't happen. Instead, the base General locked down, told the PSR to fuck off and that they were loyal to the United States of America and to the President of the United States."

"That takes some balls."

"Yeah, Scary Terry was like that. A real fighter. It's the reason I liked him. Reason a lot of the guys I knew loved him. He was a real Marine. Not a fucking politician."

"So what happened?"

"Well, the PSR couldn't have open rebellion against them, so they gathered their forces, got real buddy buddy with the

175

Chinese, and sent us in to round up the rebels. Those who signed loyalty oaths were spared. Everyone else was deemed expendable. It didn't go well. The Marines didn't like the idea of Chinese troops on American soil, so they counterattacked. Sorties were being flown from Yuma and 29 Palms until the jets ran out of fuel. Ran out of bombs first and started dropping anything heavy they could, hoping to hit something, I guess. The standing order for all American troops was to stand their ground and fight to the end."

"Yeah, we had something like that in New Jersey. But no one attacked them. Most East Coast bases ended up becoming ghost towns. Everyone just left after a while."

"Well not here. There were guns everywhere. Fucking Boot Camp platoons that had just formed up were being sent from the recruit depot to the front lines. They weren't even Marines yet. By the end, there weren't a lot of signers. I never got a good number, but a lot more either died fighting or chose to face the wall. Stenka signed. He saw me. I wouldn't be surprised if he tried to kill me if he saw me again. Figured I don't need the trouble."

Michael didn't respond, seeing that Jose had not yet finished what he wanted to say. He'd wait a while.

"I didn't like what I did to them. I didn't have any good feelings taking down the flag from the base, piling up all the Eagle, Globe, and Anchor emblems I could find, and then setting them ablaze. I didn't like the looks I got from those who surrendered, who looked like they still had all the fight left in them. They beheaded Scary Terry on a Livestream. Called it a victory celebration, but I didn't see anybody cheering. But then again, nobody stepped in to stop the thing from happening, so I guess that's a W in the PSR's column. All I felt was anger and hatred during the whole damn thing. They forced the PSR to respond and I had to do my job. I hate them for what they made me do. They were my brothers, Mike."

They were quiet for a while. It was a mournful silence, yet also one of solemn understanding. They both knew what they were and if there was an afterlife, where they'd both end up. Sins are not washed away by circumstance. Cain might have been a paragon of virtue in every other moment of his life but one. But it was that one moment, the very first murder, the murder of his own brother, that sealed his fate for all eternity. Jose left after some time, marching to a fugue that no one else could hear.

CHAPTER TWELVE

Michael was still on watch when he heard footsteps approaching. At first, he thought Jose had come back, but these steps were more labored, dragging, and at points, aimless. A few moments later, Joe was in sight, stumbling around drunk, muttering slurred curses to himself and those close enough to hear him. Michael saw him see him and the drunken ring leader made his way over to the sober sentry.

"Citzhen Connors, how the hell are ya?" he slurred.

"You're drunk, Joe. Go to bed."

"I am drunk. Very ass toot oservation. I'm drunk. You're armed. Let's go stir up trouble, huh?"

Michael, even when normal, hated the role of babysitter for the drunk. He remembered soldiers he had to nurse back to some kind of health on nights on base when the women were scarce but the alcohol flowed like the Mississippi. He hated it, but in the morning, they'd be his friends again and a different night, he knew that it would be one of them taking care of him. Perhaps Joe would remember any kindness that Michael paid him in the morning.

178

"I think we're in enough trouble already, no?"

"What? Trouble? No! Never. We're citizens of the Pacific State's Republic. Trouble's over my friend. Trouble's over." He plopped down onto the ground and fell on his back, wobbling like a weeble, but not falling down.

"You're a true believer, huh? Universal kinship, unfettered devotion to human rights, all the propaganda?" Michael asked, entertaining the drunken comrade.

"Of course! Though, I haven't gotten to really live there that long. Trouble with my line of work," he stopped for a second, then picked up a different thought, "You know it's ironic. I find paradise on Earth and am then asked to give it up to help others live a life I can only dream about. Kinda fucked, huh?"

Michael was taken aback at the coherence of Joe's point.

"I mean, I'm sure that it's got problems, but man, they ain't problems. I see real problems every day. I hear real problems all the time from you good citizens every day. Did you know that Cherry's name ain't Cherry? Of course, I mean who names a kid Cherry, right? But Cherry's name is Ashley. She told me so. She's got real problems. Not fake problems like those citizens in the PSR. She had a kid. She had a kid and no way to feed him. Now, an attractive young woman with a few assets in the middle of hell on Earth has to do what she has to do. Nothing wrong with selling whatcha got. But that kid died. He died! Got sick and then got sicker and then he died!" Joe started to sob. He watered the barren dirt below him for a few moments, then changed demeanors on a dime.

179

"That's why I believe, Connors," he mumbled, sitting with his legs crossed, like a yogi. "These people... They've all got so much hope. So much grit. They're the ones who lived. And once they get home, they'll do anything to keep it. They'll fight til the end. There are so many in the Republic who take that security for granted. They keep their heads down, do what they're told and I bet that ninety-nine hundred percent of 'em would keep their heads down if Alex Mercer rolled through. Sheep, Connors. Sheep. But you, you're a goddamn wolf. I see you and I think, 'Wow. This things gonna have some staying power.' That's the beauty of this mess. Wolves are gonna keep the thing floating. And if we lose a few sheep in the process, I won't weep for them."

"I bet you some of these people were the type to keep their heads down," Michael noted.

"All of 'em. Cept a few. But yes. But circumstances being what they were, the sheep died early. The survivors got mean. Circle of life, my friend. When the enemies come, they'll be attacking wolves."

Michael stood, thinking. He could see the blips of drones flying overhead. Michael wondered about who the pilot was. Bodies were so valuable in America, so they were probably foreign. Chinese if it was a PSR drone. Mercer was probably hiring out of India. Whoever it was had probably never thought about Iowa or the Mississippi more than once in their entire lives before they were a pilot. Now, they sat behind a screen and shot lightning from the sky as if they were Olympic gods. All for less than three dollars a day.

"What about when the wars end?" Michael asked. "And there are no more enemies. What happens to those wolves?"

"There will always be enemies. Our Republic, our society, is a great machine. And the people that make up the machines, it's not even their fault. They're just vessels for the true enemy."

"The true enemy?" Michael's eyebrow raised.

"Ideas, Citizen Connors. Dangerous ideas. Mind viruses. Memes that take on their own life. You remember the Internet. Whole political movements lived and died and were reborn. It doesn't matter how society functions. If we want to keep it going, we need to insulate it from the enemy. Like a garden trying to keep the encroaching jungle at bay. There will always be enemies. So, there must always be soldiers, Citizen Connors. And you'll be one of them, I think."

"I'm nothing more than the combination of timing and circumstance," was all he could say. He kept his eyes forward, hoping the conversation was settled and Joe was sober enough to know not to continue. He was. There was a long, welcome quiet. Was it fate that brought him to this spot? Was it destiny that castrated him? He was another cog in Joe's great machine, doing his job and fulfilling his role until time and circumstance wore him down to the nub and he was replaced by another newer, shinier cog. Meanwhile, the great machine would keep going as if Michael had never even been part of it.

Joe got up and dusted off his uniform, spat, almost gagging, "She's a special woman, you know?"

"Cherry?"

"What?" he raised his voice. "No, damn it. Not Cherry. Cherry's a worn-out hooker. Anne. Anne's special."

He unzipped his trousers and poked through the hole in his boxers. Michael, who'd seen plenty of men piss in his life, looked away, doing his best to not see another. He found it odd that Joe used the hole. No man he ever met used the hole meant for exactly what Joe used it for. He really was a man of the Pacific States Republic, where everything had a purpose and to be useful was to be godly.

"We signed up for this job together, ya know? She's a bigger believer than me," he said between streams.

"I'd marry her if she believed in that, but she's more of the everyone for everyone else sorta woman," another trickle finished and he shook with vigor.

"I like the space between rest stops. The time on the road when I'm the most appealing man in the area. She, who can have anyone, has to settle. It's fucking pathetic. But, the happiest moments of my life come right after she rolls off from on top of me and her breathing starts to slow back down and I feel like maybe now she'll wake up and see how much I love her. But then we get to towns as this and soldiers saunter around in their perfect uniforms. I do my best to keep this old thing in order, but the road doesn't have much in terms of dry cleaning. But we'll be back on the road soon and she'll be mine again, for a little while at least."

Joe zipped and headed back to camp, singing as he stumbled back and forth in one direction like a snake. He fucked up the lyrics so bad, that he stopped midway because the rhyming didn't make sense, so instead, Michael only heard, "But the Devil take the Women, cause they never can be easy" on repeat til he was too far away. It was a cold evening and Michael noticed that the ground had frozen over in some parts. Winter was on its way and there was a long-distance between the caravan and California.

A few days later, they loaded up and gathered near the ferry. They were half what they were the night before. Michael saw a few familiar faces walking around town like they'd been born and bred there. The small comforts of town life, even this town, were too alluring for most people who were just looking to get out of danger. They couldn't be blamed, but Joe snarled when he saw what remained. There went half his pay, probably.

It was a short journey across the Mississippi, but because of the horses, the Captain had to take two trips. He was old and blind and had more confidence than a man in that situation should have. He was dressed in a warm wool sweater, corduroy pants, and thick, dark sunglasses, and complained often about the cold. The ferry, which was a generous term, was a wide wooden skiff, pulled by hand across the water. So many were trying to get across, the captain demanded payment when they made it to the deepest part of the river. He wanted things from people. Precious things. Items that these people had chosen over all their other worldly possessions to take with them to their new life. But instead, those objects would part with their owners. Some were photographs. Some were expensive, gaudy pieces of jewelry. Michael was unsure what he would part with.

"These were my mother's," Cherry said, handing over an antique pearl necklace that had seen better days. With a deep cleaning and care, it would shine bright, but she hadn't the tools, the time, or desire for better days to bring herself to maintain them. The Captain held out his hand for them and she took a second, running the individual pearls between her fingers like she was praying a rosary. The Captain, like a statue, waited for her to finish her goodbye. She placed the necklace in his hand, coiling them in his rough palm, before grabbing his fingers with both hands and closing them around the pearls. He placed his other hand on top of hers and patted them, then cooly went on to the next, placing the necklace in his pocket.

Peter was next and though the boy had no possessions in the whole world, he pulled out two pennies and some lint from the front pocket of his jeans and handed them over without question. He wore an innocent smile that the blind Captain could not help but return, compelled by a force that existed outside of sight.

"What years are these?" the Captain asked, holding the pennies in front of the boy's face.

Peter looked them over and his eyes grew wide with excitement, "They're both from nineteen eighty-five!"

He started giggling at the coincidence, not sure why it was so funny, but it was infectious and soon, several of the adults were laughing along. Michael noticed this and wondered what the odds were that both pennies were from the same year. He was never great at any math outside of calculations, which he could do in his head, so he could only give guesses and lay opinions. Maybe they were made in the same mint. That was more likely.

There was only a handful of those across the country. The pennies traveled great distances in pockets and purses and perhaps even the cupholder in someone's car. And though they traveled far and wide, this was the first time they were probably used on the giving end of a transaction. It was far more likely that they were given once as change, then left to travel, changing hands by circumstance rather than part of a sale.

"My little girl was born in nineteen eighty-five. Though, she probably ain't little no more. You know what this means?"

Peter shrugged.

"Me neither, but I ain't so blind that I don't notice a sign in front of me. Here, you keep this one. Hold it tight. Remember it. Might not mean nothin'. Might just be a copper portrait of the Great Emancipator. Or, it could be magic!"

Peter took back the less shiny of the two pennies and held it up to the sky to get a better look at it. He started giggling again.

Down the line, they went like that for a while til the Captain came past Donahue, who refused to meet the Captain's vacant, but all-seeing, gaze.

"You must pay the toll," the Captain said to Donahue. "Can't get over without paying."

Donahue huffed and crossed his arms. "I don't see any point. I could hand you a quarter and tell you it was made of gold and you wouldn't know the difference."

"I wouldn't care, either, to be honest. You'd have paid something. What you pay is between you and God, far as I'm concerned. I'm just here to collect. If you think this trip's only worth that, fine by me, but I've found that those who know what lay on the other side of the river give up things they cherish, just for the chance of getting it."

"I don't need the spiritual bullshit. Especially from a blind shyster. You know what I think? I think you're exploiting these poor people for no other reason than you can. You're the bottleneck here. You get to set a price and force these saps to pay up. Well, throw me off if you gotta, but I ain't doin' it. I don't bow to anyone. I don't kiss up. And I don't say thank you after getting fucked in the ass. So what are you gonna do now?"

The Captain kept his blank expression, looking past Donahue through his thick black lenses. The hand he'd been holding out went into his pocket.

"When Cain killed Abel, he did it because Abel had found favor with the lord. He lived a privileged existence, bearing the sins of his parents and giving proper thanks and sacrifice for his precious life. Cain, well, Cain didn't. Just remember, when you don't get what you want out of life, you sacrificed nothing trying to gain everything."

The Captain moved down the line collecting treasures and trinkets from most everyone. Bobby forked over a can of his precious cat food and John handed over his watch, a cheap digital timepiece. The Captain stood in front of Michael, unencumbered by his hefty load. He put his ashen, hardened hand out and Michael noticed how deep the grooves in his palms went as if they were carved from oak. Shaking his hand would be like grating cheese.

"And what do you have for me?"

Michael said nothing and instead brought his rifle to the ready. Several of the other travelers got worried and though Michael made no attempt to conceal his motions or the sounds he was making with the rifle, the Captain stood firm, his hand still out, insistent. Michael racked back the charging handle and a round flew out of the ejection port onto the ground. He picked it up and dropped it into the Captain's hand. The captain felt it and played around with the bullet in his hands, pressing his thumb across the tip, feeling the seem where the actual projectile met the casing.

"Funny how these things don't seem so bad up close. Holding it in your hands, one could be forgiven for forgetting how dangerous bullets and guns are. I used to hunt. Long time ago, when I could still see. I remember the smell most of all. Memory works like that. Olfactory glands pass right through the memory center of the brain or something like that. The smell of burnt cordite brings it all back."

"Nitroglycerin," Michael replied.

"Excuse me?"

"Modern bullets don't use cordite. They use sawdust coated in nitroglycerin."

"Well thank you for the lesson. You must know a lot about guns, then."

"I know a little about a lot."

The Captain kept fumbling with the bullet like a gambler with his last chip.

"You know anything about huntin'?"

"Little bit," Michael spat.

"I used to hunt squirrels and rabbits, mostly," he smiled, "Sometimes, though. Sometimes, I had to hunt monsters. You ever meet a monster?"

Donahue flashed in Michael's mind. The old couple in Jersey City. Jake. Himself.

"Seems you can't move too far these days without meeting one or two, I reckon. When I was a boy, my father... He was a real monster. He didn't drink. Didn't smoke. Went to church every week. And when he'd get home from work, he'd beat the black off my mama. We lived in the middle of the woods, ya see. Nice piece of property, good for hunting and fishing and beating women. She'd scream and scream and if she didn't, he'd just go harder on her. I walked in once. She was a bloody mess. He was standing over her with this wide smile and then he beckoned me over. I left. He followed. He started screaming, too. About how I needed to learn something. When he turned the corner round the house and saw me with my varmint rifle loaded, he almost died laughin'."

"You gonna shoot me with that? Your own father? Who's gonna put a roof over your head, huh? Food in your mouth?"

188

"He said so many different things. Asked a bunch of questions. Didn't stick around long enough to hear the answer. He turned around after he figured I didn't have it in me. He was probably gonna take it out on my mama. So I yelled at him. I don't even remember what. And he turned around and I fired. Right in the eye. Great shot. He died a coupla hours later. Hunting accident it was called. Everyone in town knew about him. No one gave me any trouble about it. 'Cept Mama."

He handed the bullet back to Michael.

"All sorts out here. Things bein' as they are, this one's on me. You can get me on the way back. I have a sense you won't be out West for long."

He couldn't see through the Captain's glasses, but Michael swore he winked, then moved down the line. They disembarked on the other side of the river. They waited all day for the rest of the caravan to cross and by the time all the supplies and horses and other odds and ends were over, they'd just enough time to make camp for the evening. All night on watch, Michael saw the anti-drone batteries going off at different, random intervals. They all played out the same way. Booming shot fired, rocket noises getting softer and softer, loud explosion coupled with bright light, and a few seconds later, a large shake in the ground if the drone got close enough. Some earlier generations came with countermeasures, but the line of production got so cheap that they cost less than the missiles that could shoot them down. Deluge official policy on drone warfare was to flood the skies with scrap metal and bleed the PSR's wallet dry. That tactic got them the airspace as far as Indiana and no further than the Appalachians. Jose did not come that evening. Neither did Joe, nor the old men or the fake German. Michael was all alone underneath a wide, clear sky, watching drones explode like fireworks. Out in the distance, he saw other explosions from batteries further up and down the river. Further West, other batteries caught the few drones that made it through the first wave.

There was one kid he remembered for no particular reason, except that he was one of Michael's first recruits. He was a flyer. Michael knew he would be. He'd looked like a flyer. Most recruiters could tell who you were with a look. Flight, fight, or freeze was the mantra. The kid had probably heard a lot of stories about recruiters and they all end the same way, more or less. "That won't be me! I'm too fast, or smart, or strong, or whatever," they'd say. It all boiled down to "I'm special."

The freezers are the easiest by far, but freezers more or less didn't make it through training. Some guys got superstitious of freezers. Better to take them out then and there and write it up as self-defense. Fighters aren't nearly as tough as they thought they were, but usually tough enough to make it through boot camp, which meant a small bonus. Flyers were hit or miss. There were also those who begged for it; begged to just get it all over with then and there. Michael never obliged. Didn't make sense to. Donahue did.

Though he was often told by Captain Marcus, "Doesn't matter how they get on the bus, just that they get on the bus," Michael felt an obligation to serve up the most able-bodied men and women he could. This kid was fast, though. Ran track in high school. Michael had a whole file written up on him. In the early days, they had such luxuries. Michael remembered having a modicum of respect for that style of recruiting. It was more

190

like man-hunting than slave catching. He'd get a file, follow leads, interview people, and sometimes even came up short. There was a cat and mouse aspect that gave him a sense of accomplishment and purpose. But then Benning happened. A whole army destroyed and a mad rush to get something back into the field, fast. As fast as the kid.

"Doesn't matter how they get on the bus, just that they get on the bus." These were the words Michael heard when he pulled out his pistol. Michael stopped running and took aim. The kid, who had to be thirty yards ahead of him at this point, in the pitch-black darkness of night, was gaining distance. His file said he was a track star. Michael breathed out until all the air left his lungs and then fired. Looking up from the sights, Michael saw the kid tumble to the ground. At first, believing he'd killed his pursuant, Michael sauntered over to the body for identification and collection. The kid, who'd previously believed he was steps from freedom, was now screaming and writhing on the ground, holding his calf, bleeding on the concrete sidewalk below him. "A leg shot", Michael thought. "Thought I was aiming center mass." He grimaced as he stood over top of the kid, who couldn't have been much older than Michael when he joined the army. He looked into the kid's eyes and saw nothing but fear.

"You're fast", Michael said. "Maybe that'll keep you alive."

"Fuck, man. Why did you fucking shoot me?" the kid wailed.

"You should have shown up to your draft day."

Donahue pulled up to the scene in his vintage Cadillac as Michael was finishing up the dressing on the kid's leg. They loaded the kid into the backseat and headed for the Military Entrance Processing Station, or MEPS.

"Are you taking me to the hospital? This really hurts!" the boy writhed.

"You had to shoot him? Fucker's bleeding all over my backseats. They're leather, you know? What the fuck, Mike?"

"Army will patch you up when we get you to MEPS", Michael replied, ignoring Donahue's bitching.

"Please. Don't make me go. I'll do anything, please. I know this guy who said he isn't going to show up to his processing date. You could take him instead of me, right? Come on, man!"

He wasn't a bad kid. File said he volunteered at his church. He helped his mother run a small convenience store in their neighborhood before everything went to hell. Michael thought about the offer. It wasn't a crime to talk about skipping your date with destiny. He could talk about skipping or fleeing every day up until his number was called and until he doesn't show up, he is still a law-abiding citizen. He even gets three chances. The clerk calls out a name three times, pausing for a minute in between calls. After that third time, it was open season. Michael had seen guys come in just as their name had been called a third time and a bunch of recruiters would grumble to themselves as they crossed the name off their lists and waited, like scavengers or some ambulance-chasing lawyers, for the next no show. After a while, Michael stopped hanging around the MEPS. It was much more comfortable to wait for the list of names to reach him by the end of the day. He just worked off of previous days' lists.

"Sorry, kid. Your buddy's allowed to say whatever he wants 'til his date. Freedom of speech is the bedrock of a stable democracy, after all," Donahue replied, chuckling to himself.

When they pulled in, Michael helped the kid into a wheelchair, and then wheeled him to the front desk. The place looked a lot different when he enlisted. Where there used to be American flags and motivational recruiting posters for the different branches of the military, it was now a barren, sterile, and lifeless waiting room, void of any personality or pride. It reminded him of a computer parts factory. The kind where everything was brightly lit with fluorescents and everyone would wear gloves, masks, and hospital scrubs. A shitty airport terminal that red-eye flyers waited in between connecting flights.

"Name?" the clerk asked, not looking up from his computer screen.

"Anderson, Derek. Number 201850."

The clerk pulled up the file.

"All-county record holder, huh? No wonder you had to shoot him. Probably deserved it, too, didn't you, you piece of shit." He said, speaking to the kid. "You know how jocks can be. Picking on kids for being different." The clerk started laughing. "They don't realize that the world belongs to guys like us, now, huh?"

The clerk typed away. Michael noticed the keyboard, once white, had stained yellow from use and abuse. It looked like all manner of liquids splashed across the keys and in between the tiles were the remnants of different kinds of cheese-flavored chips or other salty snacks. The clerk, who must have weighed in excess of three hundred pounds wore thick glasses and a t-shirt for a band that Michael had never heard of. At that moment, Michael questioned what he was doing.

"What unit are you sending him to?"

"Oh, he'll be heading down South, for sure. Once that leg heals up, we'll see if he can outrun bullets. Then again, it already looks like we know the answer to that one, right buddy?", he started laughing. It was nasally and for a second it almost looked like his cheese dust encrusted fingers were going up for a high five. The look Michael gave him must have made the clerk reconsider. The clerk then cleared his throat, his voice became a little deeper, trying to grasp some professionalism.

"So yeah," he stammered, "Seems like we've got it from here. Let me just print out this slip for you and you can take it down to payroll."

"Guys like us", Michael thought as more explosions rocked overhead and the blind riverboat Captain's hunting questions danced around the hairs of his ears like a dirty secret. Derek Anderson was probably dead. But maybe he ran. Maybe he was fast enough to get to the PSR. Maybe he'd recognize Michael, even after all the years. Maybe he'd kill Michael as soon as he saw him. But he was probably dead.

CHAPTER THIRTEEN

An unforgiving wind swept across the Nebraskan plains, cutting through the shoddy tents and delivering a penetrating chill to those inside. Frozen rain accompanied the gusts and thermal imaging would show the masses of bodies look like some sort of inhuman orgy. Not the sort of thing a drone pilot would waste a shot on, but not exactly what Michael considered inconspicuous. He stood watch outside the tent about a football field away, calm, though wishing for a warmer coat. It had been about a month since they crossed the Mississippi and almost a week straight of torrential downpour. The unplowed fields around them turned into a dense soup, swallowing anything that pressed upon it with the slightest bit of force.

They learned that the hard way the other day when Johann got loose. He sprinted off, spooked by something, though no one was sure what. When he stopped, the posse that went to fetch him took their sweet time surrounding him, hoping not to frighten him further. By the time they noticed he was sinking, he was too far gone. They'd wanted to put him out of his misery, instead of letting him drown in the disparate muck that seemed neither solid nor liquid. No one had a gun on them and no one was risking his neck to kill a dead horse. When they returned, the men described his horrible whiny. Werner was one

195

of the men who went to gather the runaway. He didn't speak much after the incident, but when he did, Michael noticed he'd dropped the accent and pretenses. Abraham was pissed, but that was nothing new. Joe promised him a new horse when they got to the PSR, but his promises grew lighter and lighter as they kept going.

Above them, the air battles became more intense. Dogfighting drones flew at speeds that would force human pilots to pass out. Real-life video games. An R/C with guns. Large explosions in the sky thundered throughout the twilight horizon and were followed by the distinct sound of high speed, twisting metal that is only known to automobile test dummies and plane crash victims. Michael couldn't believe they were flying in such weather. Maybe they were flying above it? He thought. Or perhaps, without human pilots, the combatants just didn't care. That sounded likely. At that point, drones were basically free compared to pilots.

Morning came and with it, a slight reprieve from the rain. The clouds, still dark and dreary, could continue their onslaught at any moment, so the breakfast line moved fast and the hungry congregation ate with great speed and consciousness. Michael was last in line, which suited him fine since the bottom of the pot usually had the dense slop with the most nutrients. He looked haggard, his muscle tissue worn down to mere sinew and bone, his beard long and unkempt. His hair was greasy and covered in dandruff and down past the nape of his neck. He didn't look very different from the others in his unwashed mass, who'd given up on the dignity of physical appearance long before. All that mattered was the journey. The journey and the next meal.

He made it to the front of the line. The smell of boiled cardboard now a welcome Pavlovian trigger for his stomach.

"Sorry, Mike. Not much left this morning. I've got a little meat, but I think it turned," said the serving woman, whom Peter called Mom, as she scraped the bottom of the pot to make half a portion for Michael's breakfast.

"It's fine, Judy. I'll make due. I'm sure we'll pass a store or something in the next couple days. Maybe even a farm."

"You can cut out that nonsense. Name's not Judy either."

He'd made a game of guessing. To her, a playful jab to prove he was human. For him, another way to dredge up forgotten memories locked away in his castrated mind.

"Well, I'm not calling you Mom. I'll figure it out soon enough."

"Sure you will, Hun," she answered. "Or, you'll get over your Mommy issues and call me what I ask to be called."

She was stern and harsh, but still =feminine. Even emaciated, she had round warm features. Her face, weathered by age, looked like it was once as harsh and hard as her persona, but like sediment, smoothed over. Her hair was gray and thinning. Her teeth were yellow from years of social smoking, though she seemed to have kicked that habit long before May Day, given that she never ticked or jonesed like some quitters Michael had known.

"Any particular reason you wanna be called that? Or just to be special?" Michael shot back. He appreciated her hardness and found she could take a ballbusting as well as she could dish it out. Michael hadn't busted anyone's balls for some time, probably not since he was still in the Army. It was a dying art form shared between those whose closeness could weather even the most egregious, disgusting insults and insinuations. A closeness that Michael knew no longer. After May Day, he'd seen good friends at one another's throats for the smallest jab or oversight. Michael could handle himself, but saw no reason to kill a man for not taking his bullshit.

"Prison nickname," she replied.

"No shit?"

"No shit."

"That explains a few things."

"Since when are you so damn curious? Most of the time, you get your portion and fuck off to wherever. I swear, one time, you didn't even stop to get it, you just walked by with your bowl out like you was on a conveyor belt."

"Rain's got me talkative. Besides, you're finally interesting. Before now, I thought you were the female equivalent of Lurch. Or the amalgamation of every lunch lady ever conceived. You learn how to make this slop shit in prison then?"

"No, I worked in the laundry."

"So why the nickname?" Michael found himself curious and also confused at his own curiosity. Before now, he found himself not interested in much at all.

"I had a group of girls. Much younger than me. See, I was supposed to be in jail for the rest of my life. Killed my husband. He was a bastard in so many damn ways, but he didn't deserve to die. I learned that too late."

She took a second to collect her thoughts.

"I had so much time to think. learn how the system worked and I used that knowledge to try and- try and help these young girls. And not in some tutti-fruity, Kumbaya, everyone's special bullshit kinda way, either. I just did what I did and when someone asked me what I was doing, I'd tell 'em. And soon, there were a bunch of them who thought I knew what was what and we had ourselves a little family. It was nice. Real nice. I hadn't- I mean. It was new. One day, Leanne, a real uptight, smarmy kind, sees us sitting at lunch and says, 'Look at mother hen and her ugly ducklings.' I let it go on account of Leanne having four babies with four different men and I held myself above the opinions of gutter trash, but one of my girls, Rosita, she got real mad. She ran up to Leanne and was intent on rippin' her head off like a Barbie doll. Little Rosita ripped out a big old chunk of Leanne's hair and the poor thing looked like an old-fashioned friar. So, after the dust settled, I went over to Leanne and we got her all fixed up."

"How so?"

"Same way they do to you army boys. We shaved her hair and she looked like Sinead O'Connor. And the flock got a little bigger. And soon, Mother hen turned to Mom and no one was makin' fun of the name."

She stared at the ladle in the pot for a minute, like it were a portal to some distant memory.

"It was like that for a while. Then, one day, it wasn't. Lights turned out. Old rivalries got settled real quick. I ran through, shouting for the girls, tryin' ta find'em. Keep'em safe til things cooled off. But Rosita. She was so angry. I hate to stereotype, but them Latinas got a mean streak in 'em like nothin' I ever seen. She had fire. Problem child. Every family's got one. She took it out on me, on the girls, on anyone who crossed her wrong. She made more than a few enemies. When I found her, she was bleeding all over. She was crying and bleeding and blood was coming out her mouth, her hands holdin' her gut together. Wasn't long til she was gone. Horrible way to go. A couple days later, guards decided it was time to high tail it out of there and they left the doors open. I knew who killed Rosita. Thought about revenge. Everyone did. but… it wouldn't have done nothin'.'"

She looked at peace, without a hint of anger or remorse about any of it. Time did such things. Where Michael was cold and indifferent to his past, she embraced it, as if it were another orphan or lost, scared girl in her cell block. Her gaze was impenetrable and they stood in silence for a while. Where Michael would usually revel such reprieve, he found discomfort in leaving the story where she'd left it, a taste of his own medicine it seemed. That John was running up to them was a great stroke of luck, Michael thought. He'd soon regret that.

"Mom, you need to come with me," John panted, his hands on his thighs.

"What's a matter?"

"Prudence's baby's coming."

"That ain't right, she ain't due for another couple months."

"Well, either she pissed herself or the baby's coming now. You gotta help her!"

Mom turned to Michael and with a steely glare, said, "I'm gonna need your help."

She spoke with authority and Michael was compelled to follow, despite knowing nothing about childbirth, save for the circumstances that preceded the ordeal. Still, he was running to the communal tent, where most everyone was gathered outside. A hole was formed in the crowd as Mom passed through with Michael in tow. There were so many excited faces, except for Abe, who looked hungover, and Werner and Joe, who vowed to keep him sober til the baby came. Prudence screamed and cursed a storm and the thin tent walls did nothing to muffle the sound. She had a thin build and weak constitution, in even the best circumstances. Michael had her written off from day one. He was surprised to find that she roared like a lion in lamb's clothing. She screamed in both English and Dutch, as the baby came, but not in pain so much as screams of endurance. She was in a shouting match with God and she was winning, as far as Michael was concerned. She was strong. That was good. She'd need that strength. There were no doctors or hospitals around or anything else that could be counted as sanitary. She was among the last of an antiquated people, who, in better times, would be surrounded by experienced women who knew how to keep her and her baby alive. She could've afforded less courage there, but here, she'd need every ounce she could muster.

He entered the tent after Mom, letting the flap fall closed behind him. Cherry was doing her best to play doctor, while Anne was standing in the corner, unable or unwilling to move. Her hands were bloody, shaking, and she wore a thousand-yard stare. Tears had puffed her pretty face.

"This isn't right. We can't do this here. She wasn't due until we got to civilization," she mumbled, "This is impossible." She went on like that for some time and it seemed that she'd been like that for a while.

"Shut up, damn you!" Mom shouted. "You're worse than useless with that talk. Get the hell out of here if you're gonna yammer on like that." Her attention shifted. "Don't listen to her, Pru, you're doing great! So great!" Her gaze moved to Michael, "Go get as many linens as you can carry. Quickly! Cherry, dear, I've no experience in this sort of thing, so I'm gonna need you to tell me what to look for."

Cherry gave a desperate look, determined, but mired in sadness.

"I know it ain't fair, but you're her best shot, you hear me?" Mom consoled with the softness of leather.

Prudence, meanwhile, kept screaming and shouting in between deep breaths, gasping to power even louder screams

202

and shouts. She lay on the blankets the group had been sleeping on, soiled with dry sweat and now, the lifeblood of creation, mixed in with her own profuse sweat and heavy tears. Michael left the tent but was never out of earshot. He returned with the blankets, but by that time the screaming had stopped. He entered to silence, as Mom held the newborn in a swaddle made of an old beach towel. Prudence lay passed out on the ground, blood everywhere. Cherry took a spot in the corner of the tent and just sat there, the same look on her face. Anne had the sense to leave. Michael, seeing no more need for the blankets, went over to Mom and spoke in a dull whisper.

"How'd it go?"

She looked at him like he was stupid as if the evidence around him did not present a clear picture of how it went.

"Whatchu whisperin' for?" she scolded, as her hands clasped tighter around the swaddle.

"Seemed appropriate. I wouldn't want to wake Prudence... Or the baby," he answered. He was stiff, unused to tenderness of any sort. He resigned his lot in life to the taking of human life, not in bringing it into the world, and for once, he felt a warm sensation thinking about the idea that he'd added to the world, rather than taking something away from it. There was no emotion, just raw physicality, but he'd take it. It was the first inkling of a feeling he'd had in years, a major accomplishment in his mind.

"She's dead."

He looked over and it was true. Prudence, who not long before was fighting to bring her child into the world, was now another body in a land abundant with corpses. The fabric of her makeshift bed was still disturbed from her gripping and tearing, but those hands were now loose and without any motion. Her eyes were closed, with a small smear of her own blood on the lids.

"The baby?" he asked.

"He'll be joining her soon. Too small. Born too early. Real skinny. He never had a chance, I'm afraid."

"Abe?"

"I was gonna wait til after."

"Why? The man would want to meet his own son. Especially if he isn't gonna make it."

Mom fiddled with the towel and Michael understood her hesitance at once. The baby's bald, brown head poked through, too large to fit on its small, skinny body. His arms were thin and rubbery, like an old Strech Armstrong toy. He struggled to breathe and did not labor to move around much. He couldn't have been more than four pounds and he didn't make a sound.

The tent flap opened and Abe barged through, "I've waited long enough. What's going on?" There was great excitement in his eyes, though his teeth were gritting together. That excitement left as he saw Prudence's body and he returned to his cool, stoic disposition.

"And my child?"

Mom re-swaddled the baby and held it close to her, unwilling to let Abe see. "I don't-" she began, but second-guessed herself.

"He's not yours," Michael cut in. "He's-"

Abe put up his hand to silence Michael, his typical glare replaced by exhaustion. He took the swaddle and looked at the newborn.

"He's mine. My Son." Abe cradled the baby in his arms, rocking his frail body back and forth.

Mom placed her hand on his shoulder. "He doesn't have much time. He's too small. Prudence was strong-willed, but her body, it just…"

"Leave me alone with my family, please."

"Abe, I-"

"Leave us alone!" he shouted and Michael cleared the tent, followed by Cherry and after a moment, Mom.

News spread through the crowd and they dispersed, finding small tasks to occupy their time, distracting their morbid curiosity. A few hours passed and Abe emerged from the tent. He spoke aloud to no one in particular.

"I need someone to prepare their bodies. Washed and wrapped in something-", he bit his lower lip, holding back whatever was trying to come out. "Something clean."

He then marched out to the wagons, grabbed a shovel, and made for the unplowed field about thirty yards from the camp. About an hour into the digging, Mom came out of the tent and approached Michael, who'd been pretending to rest in preparation for his watch that evening. She shook the foot that hanged out the back of the covered wagon he rested in and spoke with the gentleness of sandpaper.

"You gotta talk to him. You gotta let him know what happened."

With feigned grogginess, Michael responded, "Why don't you do it?"

"I don't wanna. Cherry don't wanna. Hell, maybe we can't. You're the only one that were there that can."

"I wasn't there. I left for a minute and I came back and she was dead. It was all pretty quick. Not as quick as most I've seen, but quicker than some."

"You're a man. He's a man. Men are a confounding bunch and I don't mean to waste my time consoling a man who'll swear up and down he don't need consoling. So go talk to the bastard, will ya? I seen the look when you saw that baby. Like new life was breathed into you, too. You might not admit it, 'cause you're a stupid man like him, but you might need this, too. Idiotic sex that you are."

Michael made it to the whole with a half bottle of whiskey he'd been nursing since they left Bridgeton. He'd gotten it for the low cost of a half-full carton of Twinkies and three packs of cigarettes, which suited him fine as he hated the spongecakes and cringed at the thought of cigarette smoke. The hole was about three feet deep and while not a perfect rectangle, it was close enough. The sounds of digging filled Michael's ears as he cleared his throat, hoping that Abe would stop for a moment. He did. He looked past Michael and over to the bottle with great desire and longing, then went back to the task at hand.

"Leave it, I'll need it later."

"Thought I could share it with you."

"Great," he grunted, tossing dirt out of the hole, "idea. And while we're at it… we can… share a fatted calf… sacrifice it… and burn up my family's bodies… Sounds fun." Each pause brought more intensity in Abe's digging and large beads of sweat flew around him. There was blood on the handle of the shovel and wetness around his cheeks that went unwiped.

"I was there when she died."

He just kept digging.

"I thought maybe you'd want to know how it happened."

"I imagine there was some crying, a lot of bleeding and in the end, she just… was gone."

"She was very brave."

He climbed out of the hole, spun the shovel around, and held the spade near Michael's face. "I'll say this in language you can understand, Mr. Connors. Fuck off. And don't ever talk about my wife again. I know she was brave. She had to be to endure what she had. What do you know, huh? That woman. That woman was divine. I'll spare you the details but when the so-called recruiters came, they took more than just the able young men. I'm not stupid. I never went to a fancy school, but I know enough to know that boy wasn't my blood. But he was ours. He was going to be raised as one of us. Maybe even the last, but one of us all the same. I'm no cuckoo bird, but there are some things more important than my pride. And my wife. As close as mankind could come to angelic."

More tears came as he put the shovel down and rested against it.

"What more can I give?" he yelled. "What else do I have that you want, damn you! Take it! Take it now before I get used to having it. Please!" he cried.

Michael put his hand on Abe's shoulder and was met with no resistance.

"We were going to name him Gabriel. I think Job would be more appropriate, wouldn't you?"

"Job would do well, yes," Michael responded.

Abe jumped down into the hole and kept digging. Michael turned to leave him be when he heard Abe say something.

"We are not given that which we cannot handle. I'll endure this. Through the lord."

Michael kept walking.

"Or the bottle."

A service was held. Anne was the only one not in attendance. Joe took his spot as Eulogizer in front of the grave. A wooden cross was made and their names were carved across the middle. The loosened soil was covered in a few wildflowers that had been found nearby. Most everyone did their best to look presentable. Soiled shirts that hadn't been washed in months were tucked into mud-covered pants. Hair was combed, with fingers if nothing else. Abe stood next to the grave alone, content to bear the grief without the comfort of others.

"Our Republic," Joe began, "was founded in the wake of great social unrest. The world, as the founders saw it, was not suited for mothers and children. So it must be remade, so that every mother, every child; Can live in peace and prosperity. Prudence and Job did not get to see that dream realized. Their lives, though short, were mired in great suffering. But also, great love. The love of a devoted husband and father. The love of a devoted community. The unbreakable love between mother and child. And the love of their true home."

The service ended with no announcement. After Joe spoke, people funneled out and made preparations for dinner. As Michael was about to take his watch, he found Abe outside the covered wagon, whiskey in hand.

"So the bottle then?"

"Aye."

"Care for a drinking partner?"

"You've your duty."

"I won't drink much. It's worse to drink alone."

"Aye."

Michael climbed out the back of the wagon and slung his rifle over his shoulder, then took the bottle and drank a small swig.

"Watered down," Michael spat.

"Shame."

The pair walked out past the tents and the grave to a bit of land that was a hair higher than the surrounding land around them. There, they watched out and drank and seldom spoke except for the occasional grunt or mutter. It was a long while before Abe had enough liquid courage to speak.

"I'm ready to hear how she died. If you're ready to tell, that is."

Michael kept looking out past the campsite, unsure what to tell him. The rain started again and wouldn't let up for a few days.

CHAPTER FOURTEEN

Another horse died. He threw a shoe and broke his leg. Donahue shot him. It was fortunate for most everyone involved, save the horse, as they hadn't had a decent meal in a few days. Their foraging in the small shops and restaurants were returning less and less and it was dangerous to venture too far from the highway. They cannibalized the leftover wagon, using the spare parts to fix the others. Winter was waltzing closer and closer, whipping fierce winds and stabbing, frozen rains like shrapnel across the landscape.

Michael had found a pair of winter boots in his last scavenge that happened to fit, sewing envy and discord throughout camp. He found no gloves and felt his hands dry out and crack, looking like he'd been punching oak planks for days straight. The only hat to be found was a greasy, worn-out, red and white, Cornhuskers knit cap that looked like something Waldo would don to hide from sleuthing children. He'd found it underneath the seat of an old pickup truck with a farmer's license plate. His patchy beard fostered an awful smell, despite efforts to keep it in some sort of order.

Horsemeat stew wafted around camp for the third straight day and with it, a renewed sense of joy and pep in the camp.

211

Donahue brought out his guitar for the first time in weeks, singing old standards that kept dwindling spirits going like the small embers of a dying flame. And though the stew was more of a soup at this point, its ratio of broth to meat flipped the other way, they were thankful and fed and could go on another day. Michael trudged over to get his lunch, grateful that the stew was warm, the best compliment he could bestow on the flavorless, boiled meat and enigmatic grain dish.

He took a seat around a dim, but warming fire, whose crackling embers teased memories of warmer days. He ate fast, not liking to stay still for too long if he could help it. He sat next to Werner, who sat next to John and Bobby, who'd grown crotchety and was fighting a cold. Abe took a seat next to Michael, who'd stayed near him since Prudence and the baby. He took long swigs of whiskey from a flask he pulled out of his pocket, nudging Michael to share some with him. He always found Whiskey, it seemed. Even when there was nothing around for miles, he could sniff it out. In abandoned cars, hidden in some gas station's front counter, stowed behind a store manager's desk in the back. The largest haul was found in the freezer of a McDonald's. There were twenty full bottles of Tennessee Whiskey, and a few more half empty. So many, they couldn't all be taken, much to the chagrin of Abe and just about everyone else.

"Warmth juice," Abe said, in a dry, facetious manner. He only shared his drinks with Michael, who always declined at first, then accepted on further interrogation.

"Pass'er down, won't you? I could use a little warmth, Man," John spouted. The cold had soured his jolly persona. The hunger had muted his toothy smile and boisterous laugh. He was now again, the man who'd gone to Vietnam, or at least the one Michael conjured when listening to the stories he told. Michael looked to Abe before passing, who nodded and handed the flask over to Werner, who took his drink and passed it along to John. Bobby tried, but almost vomited at the smell and instead, curled into a ball and tried to keep warm, the cat sitting on his lap doing the same. Donahue and Cherry got their turns before Joe joined the circle and had a look of contempt at the haggard gaggle.

"Citizens, perhaps we shouldn't sloth about like this. Devoid of any pride. Any self-respect. This is not the behavior our Republic wants from its people."

"Will you shut the fuck up?" Bobby snapped. "You act like California's the land of Milk and Honey, but it all sounds like bullshit to me. Only reason we're all going along is because it has to be better than this, so just shut the hell up and tell us when we need to shove off!" He retreated into his bundle and the rest continued drinking and eating.

Joe's fury rose to the surface and he looked around as if asking the others to correct Bobby's insolence. No one stirred and he stomped off like a child who'd been sent away without dinner. His boots squeaked with every step, causing an uproar of laughter. Even Michael gave a slight, forced chuckle in solidarity.

"Is he ever not making noise?" Michael asked and they laughed. It was the first joke he'd told in some time and the looks he was getting around the campfire were warm and genial. Abe slapped him on the back as if it were the first time he'd laughed in a while. As they ate, Michael smirked. He

213

wasn't happy, he couldn't be. But the mildest form of contentment filled his person and for that moment, Michael felt human. But the moment passed and the contentment escaped him, leaving behind a real, if faint, hope that many more such moments were in his future. He'd find Daisy and then maybe stay in California. Sidney Posner was no one to him, least of all someone he felt had to die. He could be normal, or at least a version of normal. He could live with that.

So enraptured with himself, Michael only picked up Bobby's last few words, but from the tone, it was most likely more disparaging remarks about Joe. There were a few nods from the others and Bobby coughed after he finished speaking. The cat tried to remain undisturbed, readjusting after the old man calmed down.

"He hasn't been the same since we crossed the Mississippi", Werner pointed out.

"I wouldn't either if my girlfriend was fucking other men right in front of me" Donahue replied.

"What are you talking about?" Werner asked, a puzzled look on his face.

"Yeah, she's been around the block a few times. Bridgeton, One dude in Gary. Hell, she begged me to fuck her, but I don't shit where I eat. Plus, Cherry and I are happy, ain't that right?"

"Yeah", Cherry answered as she rolled her eyes and smoked a cigarette. "Every day's a fucking Honeymoon."

There was a long silence as they sat and enjoyed their stew. The biting winds subsided for the time being and there was a stark beauty in the landscape around them. The soil, whose nutrients and minerals had been sucked out decades before and kept fruitful by chemicals, additives, and pesticides, was in a state between barren and virgin. Tufts of wild grass and other weeds poked through here and there but as winter arrived, they were mostly flattened and dead.

"Maybe I'll stop here", Abe said to no one in particular. "Maybe this will be my plot of land."

"What's that?" Michael asked.

"Maybe I can start here. Build a home. This is good ground. As good as any. Maybe I'll stop here. No more English, no more riding. I could start here. Prudence and Job aren't far back. This is good ground." There was a tear in his eye that sparkled against the fire, but he wiped it away before anyone else could notice. Michael saw it and looked at the damp spot of his glove.

"Don't talk crazy, Abe", John replied, "Men out here will kill you. They think this is their territory. That our passing through is trespassing."

"What is it you English say, 'Possession is nine-tenths of the law.'"

"No law out here", John answered.

Donahue stood with a sullen look on his face. "Wrong." He looked down at Cherry with the cigarette hanging from her mouth and plucked it from her lips in one motion, its weight not yet registered as missing from her being. He took a long drag and blew upward.

"Out here is the only place where there is law. The law of strength. In society, there is consequence, sure, but no law. Laws cannot be broken. Try gravity or the speed of light. Man's laws are suggestions at gunpoint, but out here, in the land of strength, the strong eat. The weak die. Good man, bad man. Rich, poor. Holy or blasphemous, it is the strongest who survive. And once the strong have laid their claim and defended it from weaker ones, that is the pinnacle of man. The moment after supreme victory, when the invader is defeated or the invaded subjugated. There is a brief moment of Elysium, followed by a decline into weakness that you know as society."

He finished the cigarette, dropping the butt in the dirt and smothering it under his shoe, the tiny embers extinguished.

"Out here, there are thousands of Kings, and one day there will only be one. Maybe it's Alex Mercer. Maybe it's First Citizen Archer. Maybe it's some bureaucrat in China, or Russia, or Europe. I don't know. But what I do know is, I've met at least a hundred men who took some land, called it theirs, and killed anyone who tried to challenge them. They are those who shall inherit the Earth. What I mean to say is, Abe, if you can stake your claim and live, you should. It will be the greatest thing you could ever hope to achieve."

Silence, followed by the small movements of spoons against near-empty bowls filled the void where optimism once lived. Donahue stared around the camp, though none met his gaze. It was a good few minutes of panning and then he bared his teeth and bit, "You cowards. You absolute cowards. You have the world right there and only need to reach out, but you'd rather stick your heads in the sand. That weakness will kill you, bet on that."

He grabbed Cherry by her arm and dragged her to her feet. "Come on, I want to show you something", he told her with a smile. A look of horror flashed in her eyes before a welcoming smile washed over her face. She took him by the hand and led him away towards the tents.

Michael came near the end of his portion and held the bowl to his lips, downed the remains, and wiped his mouth with his sleeve. As he went to stand, Werner grabbed at his shirt, a smile on his face, as if he'd just invented electricity.

"What are you gonna do when we get to California, Mike?"

"What?"

"Well, if Abraham is going to stay here, I figure we all should let him know what he's going to miss out on. What will you do?"

"Find my sister."

"Yeah, but after that. I figure that'll take a week at most. But it's a long life afterward, I hope."

"I don't know."

"I'm going to find my son", John added. "His kids should be grown by now. He might even be a grandpa."

217

"How old are you?" Werner asked.

"Old. Good diet and exercise. Lotta sun on my face. Plus, The Grateful Dead keeps me young in mind, body, and spirit, man."

John smiled. "My son played football. He liked the Cincinnati Bengals, closest team to us. I didn't like sports. My wife," he smirked, "She thought sports were too commercialized. Football was too violent. I agreed with her, of course. But he loved it. Used to beg me to throw the ball to him. I wonder if he'd be up for a catch when I see him."

There was more silence after and Michael left to start his watch.

"You never answered my question", Werner pointed out and Michael turned around.

"He'll work on my homestead when I get it in California", Abe butted in.

"I thought you were staying here."

"No whiskey here", he said with a wink. There was more laughter and Michael nodded, walking off into the distance.

That night, Michael and Jose walked a spiral-like path around the camp, going out further and further into the night, keeping their eyes on the unknown beyond the perimeter of their owned space. Everything to his right, he thought, was his and was safe, everything to his left, was theirs and unsafe, but every step out into their territory was an invasion and became his and he stood a bit straighter knowing that he'd imposed himself upon the world, unmolested.

It was around three AM when Michael saw the rising smoke obscure the full moon's shine. He and Jose dropped to one knee, then move like field mice across the open plain to find a better vantage point. A small rise in the landscape provided the best view and they scurried over on hands and knees, careful not to alert any scouts to their presence. Michael figured they would already be dead if the opposite were true, as it would be easy to kill two guys walking and talking in the middle of the night.

They spotted a small town, more a collection of hasty constructed buildings and shacks and a roaring fire at the center of it. They had no cars or horses and the proximity to the Platte River made it seem that it was a town or at least the beginning of one. There were four longhouses that could fit about twenty people or so each. There was a chicken coop, a pigpen, and stables for at least three horses.

"I'll keep an eye out here, you go back and tell Joe", Jose ordered and Michael scurried back to camp, a few miles away, to let the others know what they'd happened on. He opened the flap to see Joe and Anne laying naked together and after the shock had worn off, Michael went ahead with his report, much to Anne's chagrin, who made little effort to cover herself but looked incredulous all the same.

"Get Donahue", he said, "I want to check this place out. Anne, get a gun and keep watch. If you hear gunshots, get everyone up".

She pouted, huffed, and dressed, grabbing a pistol from her pack that she was in no way able to hold straight, let alone fire with any degree of accuracy. She stood outside the tent, leaning to one side and wearing an annoyed look on her face. Michael went to Donahue's tent and heard the sound of flesh slapping against flesh.

"Donahue, somethings up. Joe wants you to come with us to check it out."

"Fuck off, I'm busy", he replied as Michael opened the flap and found Donahue on top of a blue-faced Cherry, struggling to get any sort of oxygen. Donahue turned his attention away and a mix of shame and fury came across his face. He let go of Cherry, who started choking and gagging for air.

"Unless you want to hit it from behind, get the fuck out of here."

Michael closed the tent and the sounds of pounding flesh on flesh continued, this time at a harder rate. He met back with Joe and the two found Jose. Joe was sweating, his eyes wide as he counted the longhouses and saw how big their fire was. There were no weapons that he could see, but the slight twitch he made as he reached for his pocket told Michael that he was scared and about to do something drastic.

"These people are enemies of the state. Com-Combatants against the Republic. We need to do our duty".

"It looks like a village. They might even help us if we go about it the right way."

"We don't need help", he screamed in sotto-voce and pulled out a cell phone. It had been some time since Michael had seen one, but the black mirror box was unmistakable. It looked new, but somehow in the decade since he'd last used one, they hadn't changed at all. Small enough to fit in a pocket, minimal buttons, and a touchscreen that could crack if it met resistance from an uncooked grain of rice. The screen lit up and Joe typed away, a quaint novelty from a bye-gone era in Michael's mind. After his fiddling, Joe put the phone away. A few moments passed and from the distance, the blinking lights of a low flying drone came into view, heading right for the longhouses.

It was quick and loud and thorough, strafing the ground 4 or 5 times and implanting the soil with bullets the size of Pepsi bottles, shredding everything that impeded its journey. The mechanical belching sound the drone made was like that of an A-10 Warthog, a sound well known by soldiers in deep shit. The concept was the same. Put wings on a huge gun and point it at whatever needed to go away forever. The charming longhouses were rubble. The chicken coop and pig pen were a broken slaughterhouse. At least three horses were in pieces.

Joe and Jose walked back to camp. Michael stayed behind bearing witness to the murder. There were no screams of agony. No cries for one more moment of life. Instead, the crackling of fire and the silence of wandering ghosts, scattered across the plains by indifferent winds. Michael went to the ruin, searching for bodies, but found very little. He thought that maybe no one was in the camp at all, but knew that sort of naivete was reserved for children and expecting mothers. People had been here, there were bits of their lives strewn about the wreckage. A cast-iron pot with a large bullet hole through the bottom, a child's doll scorched, a blood-soaked sneaker, its owner still occupying it.

He approached one of the longhouses, itself the least damaged of the three, but that was like calling Nagasaki the least damaged of all cities struck by atom bombs. He saw a body in the wreckage and before he could get to it, he was tackled to the ground. It was a man who hit him and the flickering light of the flames showed Michael it was a young man, maybe even a teen. His punches were soft, tennis balls against a brick wall. And then, the training kicked in. A few maneuvers and the kid's head was locked in a vice of Michael's bicep and forearm. He hadn't even had time to think before he snapped the kid's neck. It was so easy, like opening a jar. The kid went limp and his eyes stayed open and Michael placed him on the ground with care, staring at his hands. He hadn't noticed the scratches on his arms, but they were deep and bleeding and they dripped onto the ground and the kid, whose fingernails were filled with bits of skin and blood. And he heard the drone above, readying itself to make another pass. And he made no attempt to hide from it.

CHAPTER FIFTEEN

Michael spent the day digging. Deeper and deeper, he dug, piles of earth around the plot. So many bodies to bury. A mass grave would be easier, but they deserved more than that. His hands, cracked and dried from the cold, stiff air were bleeding around the splintered wooden handle of the long spade, soaking and dripping. The deep scratches in his arms were bandaged with an old t-shirt, looking like he'd plunged them fist first into some industrial machinery. If enough time passed and he had enough blood, he was sure that the wood would stain forever. His hands, catching splinters from the shovel, fused him to the tool, one useless without the other and the other useless without the former. He'd always been a tool. A machine, built and rented to the next paying customer. It was an existence he'd come to terms with because he thought there was nothing else for him. And when he thought he could be more. When he thought he could strive for something greater, he received his reminder. His sins could not be washed away with a joke and some shallow smiles.

The strike was sudden, not long after the first. Michael had been investigating the remains of the longhouses when more bursts of fire were thrown from the sky and the awesome explosions that followed in sequence finished off whatever might have still been alive. The rounds were smaller as if the flying gun had run out of the larger caliber stuff on his first go around. He braced for the hit, thought about using the kid's body as a shield, but only for a second. Instead, he stood, waiting. And waiting. The drone opened fire, unloading its payload down to Earth and Michael welcomed it. But the shots hit somewhere else and he felt over his body for wounds and found none. There was an explosion back towards camp.

Michael rushed back to camp to find the massacre. Retaliation. Mission Adjustment. A trigger-happy drone pilot. Karma. Whatever the reason, the caravan heading West had been targeted and destroyed like a wave crashing over a sandcastle. Michael was now alone in every sense. There was nothing left to do but dig.

He first found the woman that everyone called Mom and the boy, Peter. She was sitting in their tent, a book in one hand and the boy on her lap, held by the other hand. They'd been killed by the same bullet, through their chests, with exit wounds that looked like they'd been hollowed with ice cream scoops. He buried them together, as they belonged together. They went through the world to find one another and Michael thought of his mother and the boy he'd once been and how he wished she died before she'd seen what he later did become like his father was lucky enough to do. He never learned to woman's name, but honored her wishes and buried her as Mom and got over the discomfort the name stuck in him. It wasn't her fault he had issues and she was more maternal than most women he'd met. The boy's penny was still in his pocket and Michael thought about taking it with him. Instead, he clasped it in the boy's hand and was careful with the dirt as he piled it on them.

There wasn't much left of John or Bobby, but the cat was still alive and that would have made them both happy. Michael debated taking the cat with him but he was bad with the beasts and this one tried to scratch him when he got near her. She was tough and old and had lasted much of her life alone and was probably happier without the need to care for people and Michael understood the sentiment. She groomed herself for a while and Michael petted her back, which she accepted and arched in approval. There was a can of cat food left unopened and Michael cracked it open, leaving it on the ground for her. She approached with caution, giving it a sniff, then turned around and ran off into some tall grass. He did grab the iPod, which stayed intact to his surprise. He was sure that John would want it that way. He didn't know most of the grandpa bands on the ancient device, but it was still a long road to Denver and maybe he'd learn to like something on there.

Abe had died long before, his drunken corpse moving forward each day and it was better that he die, joining his wife and his people with the God they spent their lives praising. Abe's body was far from his tent on the edge of their encampment and was in good shape relative to many of the others. By the way he was splayed out, it looked like he'd been running from tent to tent, trying to help. This was unlikely, but Michael still chose this version of events, as he wished for his friend to be redeemed.

He found Jose, still breathing, and he sighed in relief. He was in rough shape, more holes than the titanic, but he was conscious. Unsure what to do, Michael only held Jose's out-stretched hand.

"What's your sit-rep, Marine?" Michael chided.

"Leg's broken. Probable internal bleeding. Probable concussion. But at least I still have my winning personality."

Michael tried to smile to reassure him, but Jose shook his head.

"No fake shit, Mike. No more lies. No more pretending, okay?"

"Okay."

"I didn't want to die like this, Mike."

"No one wants to get shot to shit and blown up."

"Not what I meant. I didn't want to die like this."

"I know", was all he could say back.

"Don't you go this way, okay? I don't care what you have to do, but you find a way to fix yourself and you die like a man. Not a machine. Okay?"

"Okay."

"If there is a God, maybe I'll get to be me again. Even for just a moment. And then they can send me to Hell. Maybe that would be my punishment, even."

And he fell away before Michael could respond. He was a friend, too, and Michael remembered why it was better not to have them at all. He didn't get to tell Jose about the joke or the smirk or the brief feeling. Jose would've liked to have heard that. He tried to bury Jose with honors, but they had no flag and less than twenty-one rounds for the rifle. But he saluted after and made sure the cross stood up straight, even a little straighter than the others.

Donahue was still alive. He was naked, burnt, and covered in blood, but otherwise looked fine. He wandered around the smoldering debris in a daze and looked more human than he'd ever been. He shuffled past Michael, without noticing him, walking back East, limping, his left leg dragging behind the rest of his body. It was cold outside, but Donahue didn't seem to notice, instead, his gaze on the horizon, and his jaw slacked open like a country yokel.

"Donahue? Donahue!", Michael ran over and grabbed him, shaking some sense into him, "You alright?"

"No."

"You hit?"

"No." The blood was splattered over his chest and thighs, but there were no wounds that Michael could see.

"What then?"

"She's dead."

"They're all dead."

Donahue looked around and the realization came across his face in a flash.

"They're all dead. Oh my God", and he fell to his knees. He was so different. Michael was sure the old Donahue didn't care about Cherry or anyone else. He was surprised to learn that Donahue cared for him at all, even considered him a friend. His best friend, which was the height of surreality.

"What happened to you?"

"I don't know. I feel. I don't know, but I feel different. We were- We were fucking. Same as usual. She was on top of me, she had a cough from my choking her. I never heard the shots fired, but her tits exploded all over my face and her pussy contracted so tight, I came right then. Right as she died. Covered in blood and bone and her right tit and- and bits of her heart, I think, they were all over me. She blocked all the bullets and I just came. Full body. It was the most intense orgasm I've ever experienced, Mike."

He started crying, which Michael was sure he'd never see Donahue do.

"I- I can't do this anymore. I don't want to anymore. I know we had a job, but I can't. I just need to go. I just- I need to go, okay? Is that okay with you, Mike?"

"Yeah, it's okay. Go on, get out of here." Donahue walked East and kept going without looking back once and a few hours later he was no longer in the distance.

He buried Cherry's remains and had little to remember her by. She was a woman who knew the score in this world. She did what she had to do to survive and like the rest of them, had many pieces of her die off long before the drone finished the job. Michael would remember her if only because he was sure not many others would. Werner looked like he was asleep when the strike happened and was struck in the head, probably just as everything started happening. He got it the easiest.

He buried the two bodies he found from the longhouses. He wasn't as gentle as he was with his own, but he tried to be respectful. The kid was brave. He buried them in the same grave. He was tired and their graves were a bit shallower than the others and he knew it wasn't right, but he buried them like that anyway. Sergeant Ross was back and the disappointment on his face did not stop Michael from his shortcuts. He couldn't feel guilt, even if his psyche wanted him to. He thought at least that was lucky.

Joe was right outside Anne's tent, she under the covers with another one of the men from camp, but Michael couldn't identify him, his body disfigured and mangled like a car after impact with a semi-truck. A fitting end for her and Joe. One more cuckolding before their demise. Joe had been in love with her and it was that jealous rage that he could never unleash on her that sealed the village's fate and therefore their own. Joe was breathing, unconscious, and though in rough shape, he'd probably live if attended to, that wasn't going to happen. A sense of justice rushed through Michael's veins and he prepared one more grave for their coyote, who promised to get them to California, but only ensured they died without dignity or purpose. When he woke, Michael was standing over him, rifle in hand pointed at Joe's face.

"You need me", Joe reasoned. "They won't let you into the Republic without me. It's an insurance policy. I can you in, still, Citizen Connors."

"You need to come to terms. I'm going to kill you."

"What the fuck? Why? You didn't care about these fucking people? You couldn't have. I know what you are. What they made you. I knew all along. And I could have killed you, yeah. Yeah, I could have or at least have someone do it. But I didn't. That's got to count, right."

Michael didn't reply, un-shouldering the rifle for a moment, before regaining his resolve. It didn't matter that Joe knew. None of that mattered. They all probably knew. And maybe if Joe were a Rep, then they'd all still be alive. And he didn't care, at least not like they cared for him. But he wanted to care. He wanted it more than anything. Jose wanted to care, too, and now never could. Abe wanted to live his remaining days in peace, as did John and Bobby. Mom wanted Peter to grow up well and Peter wanted her to be his mother. They all wanted things and now could not have them, and Joe was their leader and it was only right and proper that he go down with them. Michael fired and Joe slumped. And it was done and Joe was buried. Michael covered the graves and marked them with what he had and did well to ensure they would last for some time, but it was more likely that a few months would pass and any passersby would not even know that people lived there, let alone were killed and buried there. That was nature and there was nothing to be done about it. It was what it was.

Michael stood in front of the graves and it started snowing and his body was weak, but he stood tall and eulogized the fallen that he let down the night before. As much as it was Joe's fault for killing them, it was Michael's job to keep them safe. Sergeant Ross was standing across the graveyard, but instead of indigence or shame, there was sadness in his eyes and something close to pity, but without judgment.

"It's not your fault", Ross said.

"I know, but it was my responsibility."

He remembered Tehran, going house to house, from street to street. The rest of his unit had gotten the surgery by this point, he was the last hold out. He never liked peer pressure and the more they tried to get him to do it, the more he resisted. Renner thought he was a pussy and they'd fought a few times and Michael had won, but Renner had gotten his shots in, too. Only Sergeant Ross had his back, it seemed.

"Connors is a big boy and if he got the ETP, he'd put me out of a job. Leave him be", and that was the final word on the whole ordeal. When he stepped on the pressure plate, Michael knew he'd fucked up. He kept his foot planted firm on the depressed metal plate, but the explosion went off anyway. The room was bright and loud and when he could see and hear, he wished he couldn't as the walls were decorated with his friends and Sergeant Ross. And when Michael got back home, he got the surgery and had his own squad and went back to Iran, never to come home fully human again.

"You didn't deserve to die. I'm sorry about that", he said to the makeshift crosses and disturbed dirt. He looked down at his feet, unwilling to face reality. "I don't know what else to say. I wish it was me instead." And then, he looked up, and Sergeant

Ross was gone. And he felt guilty, a deep-seated, anguishing guilt that rushed through his body, like blood was no longer getting to his extremities. He sat on the ground for a while, mired in shame. He cried real tears for the first time in so long and it overwhelmed him so, that he wished they were gone again, but that thought went away and he took solace in his humanity. However painful it was, it was good.

EPILOGUE

Michael had been Sean Thornton for weeks now. His new ID read Sean Thornton. His 'Babel' account was linked to the name Sean Thornton. Sean Thornton had no history before Michael called himself that at the Registry. They gave him papers, a few bucks, and a flight to San Francisco. He told them he'd been a plumber in the past. Plumbers were valuable. Their world was full of coders, bankers, artists, but so few plumbers, electricians, or anyone that could work with their hands. Even if he hadn't gotten lucky and been sent to San Francisco, he had a plan to just keep walking until he got there. He walked from Nebraska to Denver after the drone strike. When a PSR patrol found him, he'd been steps from death, collapsing on the blacktop and nursed in hospital for a week. They cut his hair, shaved him, and bathed him and he looked more like a person again.

He wasn't used to seeing people in cars, talking on cell phones, riding in buses. His heart raced as fast as his departing plane down the runway. Flying was so foreign to him, though he'd done it many times before. The world was fast again and he found himself lagging behind. Society mostly automated, yet he did things manually. The self-service shuttles stopped to pick him up, yet he walked and the autonomous vehicles, unprepared for such an event, followed him as he walked down the vacant

233

sidewalk, causing the first instance of traffic in quite some time. He kept looking out for drones, but only saw birds in the sky. Everywhere he looked, there was green grass. Water fountains. A halal cart on every corner. He didn't like scanning his ID every time he entered a building but liked less, the implants that people got to get around such inconveniences. Ocular scanners were around, though expensive and he was told that only government buildings used them.

He found work as a plumber's assistant. It didn't even matter that he knew less about plumbing than computer programming. He said the first useful job that came to mind upon entering and that became his track. He might have been the worst Plumber on Earth, but he was still to be known as one. He helped out Stavros, who never shared his last name. The old Greek had lived in San Francisco for decades and spoke of 'Okies' like they were vermin.

"You're worse than useless, Okie", he'd say to Michael. "Be careful I don't fire you. Then what will you do? They'll put you on a farm and you'll pick fruit for the rest of your life."

He didn't mind. All he did was say, "Yes, Citizen Stavros." Which pissed him off even more.

Finding Daisy was easy enough. Anyone could find anyone in the PSR. The records were immaculate and unlike other sorts of regimes, they were free and open to the public. A citizen's darkest secrets were laid bare for his neighbors to see. Every traffic ticket, every social media post, even pornographic tastes, and preferences. Babel collected it all and Michael figured that kept most people in line. Law, he noticed, was a less concrete set of rules and more a loyalty test. The most loyal citizens could get away with everything short of murder, yet even that was up for debate depending on if they "forwarded the cause" or other such nonsense handwaving.

He researched her profile, finding out everything he could about her. She was a party member and she married a bureaucrat, apparently well connected, and they lived nearby Stanford where she was an administrator. She had two children and their names were private, as was the law for under-aged people. The husband seemed decent, but not her type. He was small and he remembered that she was larger than life. Time may have changed that, as he remembers himself being open, honest, and caring at one point.

He found her house and hoped she was in that day, knocking on the door. There was no answer. He knocked again and saw a curtain flutter in the window nearest him. He knocked again, this time saying, "Daisy Connors. Daisy Connors, open up." His voice was dry and gravely and he was sure she wouldn't recognize it. It was likely she could stare him down and never guess how she knew him. He was fine with that. He knew of no other way to be.

"Daisy Connors, it's about your mother. Please open up."

This caused some shifting and after a few moments of locks un-tumbling and knobs turning, the door cracked open and half of her face poke through. She cut her hair short, almost boyish, and dyed it lighter, though not unnatural looking. There were hints of bags under her eyes and light crow's feet starting to set in. Her eyes were still hazel and there was very little she could do to change that.

"What do you want?"

"Your mother asked me to come here."

She got a skeptical look. "Yeah, and how do you know-" was all she said before the skepticism turned to joy. "Michael", was all she got out before she swung open the door and put her arms around his neck, burying her face into his shoulder like she did when they were younger. Like a hand in glove, her face fit into his shoulder, as she'd done hundreds, if not thousands of times before, and although the action was foreign to him, the muscle memory took over and he was hugging her back for a moment before going back to business.

"My name is Sean Thornton. Can I please come in?"

Confusion set in and she led him inside. They took a seat on a sofa in a tasteful, if minimalist living room. It was a stark white room with matching furniture. The couch he sat in was firm, seldom used. There was no evidence of pets or children though he knew that the two kids existed and there were pictures of her and a Golden Retriever named Roscoe. No artwork, no toys strewn about. Nothing outside of its place. It was unlike the Daisy he knew and he could tell that like their mother, she was an inmate in a luxurious prison. He'd hoped better for her, but figured she'd be dead and was unsure if this was the better outcome. She brought him a glass of water and took a seat on the adjacent couch, tears forming in the crevices of her face.

"How did you get here?"

"I walked."

"How long did it take you?"

"All together? Eight months."

"You look good."

"You don't."

She looked offended and the tears started streaming down her face. "What the hell is wrong with you? I don't see you in years and you talk to me like I owe you money? What is this", she gestured up and down his body. "What happened to you? Where is my brother?"

"My name is Sean Thornton. Your mother asked me to come find you. Michael Connors is dead. He died in a drone strike on his way out here. He'd been dead for a long time before that. An explosion in Iran killed him. I'm new to the Republic, but I do know that it does not behoove people to lie and that Babel has a way of knowing things. I also know that if Michael Connors did come here, he'd be treated as an enemy of the state, and those who knew him would be under suspicion, even those who hadn't seen him in many years."

"Sean Thornton", she whispered. She nodded her head and gave a small laugh. "The Quiet Man. Dad's favorite movie."

"Coincidence."

"What did my mother want?" she asked, in between tears.

"She's dying. She wanted me to bring you to her before she died. Seeing all this, I know it's impossible, even though I know you want to go. And after what I saw getting here, there is no way you'd survive the return trip. I doubt I will survive it."

She spilled her glass and put her hands over her tearful face. The water soaked the white carpet below her feet and she made no effort to move them out of the puddle.

"I shouldn't have come here. I think only made things worse." He got up to leave, patting his hands on his knees, a habit he learned from their father, which only made her cry more.

"No, no. Please. Please stay. For a long time, I'd hoped that my mother and brother would come here. Paul told me that it was unlikely. He's a… good man, but can be cold." She did her best to dry her eyes and the mascara started to run down her face.

"I resigned that they died and imagined horrible things. Eaten by cannibals, violated, and dragged in the streets. The news from out East is scary and almost unbelievable. I don't know many refugees, but they say much the same. They told me starving is the worst way to go. Because it's just waiting. And fading."

She paused, her feet still in the soaked carpet. "I'm- I'm just glad that you found me. I want you to meet the kids but they're at school. It all works so differently now. It's more like boarding school. Like they're the Republic's children and I just gave birth to them and-"

He cut her off before she said something she could not take back.

"She wrote you a letter. I don't know what it says. I doubt it's anything bad. She mostly reserved her venom for me. She loves you and misses you and she'll die happy knowing that you're alive. Happier when she learns she's a grandmother. What are your children's names?"

"Delilah and Michael."

"Those are fine names. Your husband was kind to let you name your children after your mother and father."

"And my brother."

"Him, too."

"It was the only thing I fought for in our marriage. He was so surprised that I asked, he let me have that. I love my children and he is their father, so I love him, too."

"But…"

"But nothing. As you said, I'd hate to say anything I couldn't take back."

The front door opened and Daisy hid the letter in between the couch cushions as her husband walked into the living room, seeing his wife in tears and Michael sitting opposite her.

"Can I help you, Citizen?" he said with politeness and an underlying threat of force.

"Paul, darling, this is my-" she stopped herself. "This is my friend, Sean Thornton. We grew up together in New Jersey. Sean just immigrated from back East and found me. He told me my mother and brother are dead."

He walked over and hugged her, holding her head in his hand and stroking her hair. "Oh, darling, I'm sorry to hear that. I told you that it was unlikely they lived. It's so awful out there, as I'm sure Citizen Thornton told you. At least now you know."

He looked down at the floor, noticing the spilled water.

"I guess you made a mess, better go get a towel to dry it up, hmm?" he asked, though sounding more like a command.

Michael stayed sitting until Paul let go of her, turning his attention to his guest and Michael stood to shake hands. Daisy crept off to the kitchen, still crying.

"Citizen Thornton, welcome to the Pacific States Republic. You must have had a harrowing journey. I'm glad you made it here safely." He spoke like a politician and his eyes told Michael to leave. Daisy shouldn't have married him. There was nothing anyone could do about that though and perhaps it was best to live in a prison of your own making.

"Would you like to join us for dinner?" he asked with the same restrained politeness.

"No. I have to be going. I have some business to attend to. Thank you for the offer."

He got up, tapping his hands to his thighs just like their father did and he made for the front door. Daisy followed him and opened the door for him. He turned as he left.

"He seems dutiful. I hope he's a good man. I know from my time back East that the less than good are not very lucky. Accidents follow them, I've heard at least."

It was a muted promise. It was the only way he could tell her that he'd kill her husband if she wanted it. She shook her head. "I love my children. I love my husband."

"Goodbye, Daisy."

"Goodbye, Michael", she whispered, biting her lip to hold back tears, before straightening herself out and returning inside.

He thought about staying. He thought for a moment that he could live a normal life. He wasn't normal, but he could try. Maybe he could learn. Maybe he could fake it until he was just thought of as a nice, quiet, peace-loving man, come to forget his troubles. But there was still the mission. Maybe it was the ETP or some small sense of duty, but he felt compelled to finish what he started. He thought of the group and the guilt that still washed through him.

It took him two weeks to track down Sidney Posner, who had no Babel account. He'd moved work camps a few too many times for the paperwork to keep up with him. He was hiding as a forced laborer in the Salinas Valley, in a work camp known as the Cabbage Patch. Michael forewent any stealth and decided the direct approach would work best. He might even be able to escape without suspicion. Maybe even getting back to Daisy and giving Sean Thornton a true chance at living. He felt a foreign sense of hope that lived in his chest and had its own yearning to break free. That had fooled him once and he did his best to temper it.

One evening, Sean came to the Cabbage Patch, with false orders to look over the cisterns. He watched Sidney Posner with great interest, trying to find out why anyone would want him killed. He was by every metric, unremarkable. He was much more fit than the old photograph Michael had gotten in the briefing, but there were still the remnants of fat around his mid-section. He was a hard worker, but not what the others referred to as 'Stans', which they'd taken from an old Russian word that Michael couldn't pronounce. He ate with the non-workers in the camp, political prisoners that the PSR hid from society. After a few days of observation, Michael went to Sidney's shack, knocking on the door, and found Sidney ready with a shiv in hand that he'd made from a screwdriver.

"Who are you and what do you want?"

"Alex Mercer sent me to kill you, but I don't want to."

"Would you like to come inside?"

Michael was sure now that Sidney Posner had indeed lost his mind those years before. "Sure. It's cold out tonight."

Michael sat on a stool near a wood-burning stove. The shack was sparse. A stove, a stool, a bedroll, and a milk crate with an antique radio on top of it.

"What's with the radio? Family heirloom?"

"Something like that. Now, if you don't mind, why don't you want to kill me?"

Michael went over the story and after a few hours of nodding and active listening, Sidney stood and asked Michael to leave.

"I'm happy here. I have my reasons just as you have yours. Please, go out and be Sean Thornton. I'd say you've more than earned it."

"He'll send more. He's determined. And that computer wants you bad. I think he'd nuke the whole PSR just to kill you."

"I waited a long time for THEO to wake up. I wish I was there to stop it. Alex was always greedy. Stupid bastard. He doesn't know what he's done."

"I liked the story, but it didn't have any knights in it", a voice called from the other side of the room. Michael saw no one but knew it was a child who called out. He only saw the radio.

"What was that?"

Sidney let out a long sigh and rubbed the bridge of his nose with two fingers. "We talked about this, Charlie. We don't talk to strangers."

"He's not a stranger, he's Michael Connors. Disguised as Sean Thornton. Here to assassinate you, but he doesn't want to. I think he's tired. I think I know him pretty well. I know him

243

better than almost anyone I know, except you, Dad. Mostly because I don't know anyone else."

Michael was confused and felt uneasy on the stool.

"Mister Connors, please meet my son, Charlie."

"He's a computer."

"Something like that."

"He's alive."

"Something like that. You seem pretty sure. How do you know?"

"Something in the voice. I just know", Michael replied. He took a moment to wrap his head around the idea. "This changes things, Sidney."

"I suppose it does." He noticed Sidney gripping the shiv tight.

"There's no need for that. I want to help you."

"Curious. To me, it seems like you'd be the last candidate to want to help us."

"THEO said something similar. Like I was a chess piece. I want to help you because-", he trailed off. He thought of Peter and the others. He thought about Daisy. His mother. He thought about his scrambled brains and what something like Charlie might do for him. Sergeant Ross would help them, he was sure of that. Donahue wouldn't and that was reason enough to help. But there was one reason that trumped the rest in his mind, in his soul, at least the parts that he could access. "I've seen a man turned into a machine. I need to believe that a machine can be turned into a man."

It was late and Sidney suggested they pick back up in the morning. Michael slept on the floor that night and when the sun rose, he felt its warming beams bathing his face. He turned over and grumbled, feeling like sleeping in a bit longer.

Printed in Great Britain
by Amazon

85279005R00142